# Jake lunged out of his chair and hit the linoleum floor with a thud.

Peter shut his eyes as Jessie scooped up the toddler. "I'm so sorry. I shouldn't have taken my eyes off him."

Jessie's heart ached for Peter. "I should have warned you he likes to jump."

What had she been thinking? She'd been selfish and smug trying to show Peter he couldn't be a parent. He *was* a parent. A parent who wanted to know his son and for his son to know him. Didn't every child deserve to know his daddy?

She'd die before she'd give Jake up. But that didn't mean she couldn't *share* him, did it?

"He could have gotten seriously hurt," Peter said miserably. She saw defeat in his eyes, defeat she'd wanted.

She felt terrible. Peter didn't deserve this. She'd been wrong.

"He won't get hurt, Peter. Not if I teach you."

## *CAROL VOSS*

Always an avid reader with a vivid imagination, Carol grew up in Smalltown, Wisconsin, with church ice-cream socials, Fourth of July parades, summer carnivals and people knowing and caring about everybody else. What better backdrop for heroes and heroines to fall in love?

In the years between business college and a liberal arts degree, Carol worked in a variety of businesses, married, raised two sons and a daughter and did volunteer work for church, school, Scouts, 4-H and hospice. An award-winning author of family stories, Carol couldn't be happier that *Instant Daddy* found a home with Love Inspired Books.

Carol lives near Madison, Wisconsin, with her creative husband, her sweet, vibrating border collie and her supervisory cat. Besides writing, she loves reading, walking her dog, biking, flower gardening, traveling and, most of all, God, home and family. She loves to hear from readers at carol@carolvoss.com.

# Instant Daddy
## Carol Voss

*Love Inspired*

Recycling programs for this product may not exist in your area.

™ LOVE INSPIRED BOOKS

ISBN-13: 978-0-373-87672-3

INSTANT DADDY

www.LoveInspiredBooks.com

**Printed in U.S.A.**

When I am afraid, I will trust in you.
—*Psalms* 56:3

To Ann and Gil

# Chapter One

When I am afraid, I will trust in you
—Psalms 56:3

Why Peter had assumed Jessie Chandler would enjoy the limelight as much as her twin sister had, he didn't know.

She stood as still as the lectern beside her, with her focus frozen on Peter's lower jaw, the toddler she'd been holding when Peter had called her to the stage asleep in her arms.

Stage fright. Great.

He glanced at the red-robed graduates sitting in front of the makeshift stage. Beyond, a sea of relatives and friends lined the football-field bleachers. Watching. Waiting.

Jessie's parents perched in the first row, seemingly holding their breaths right along with him. He was sure sitting through the memorial to Clarissa was tough enough for the Chandler family. She was killed in the New York lab fire only a year ago. The grief over losing Jessie's twin still had to be raw. And now by calling

Jessie up on stage to present the scholarship in Clarissa's name, Peter had made everything worse.

Just another reminder that he understood equations and hypotheses a whole lot better than he understood people. He sure never understood Clarissa.

He brought his attention back to Jessie.

Her gaze was still locked on his lower jaw, her eyes even bluer up close. And behind her stage fright, he sensed a compelling sadness that made him want to take her in his arms and comfort her. The breeze whipped her shiny golden hair around her face. She adjusted the sleeping toddler in her arms.

Why had she carried the boy to the stage with her? What if the kid woke up and started screaming or something? Wasn't Peter just thinking things couldn't get more awkward for the family? A screaming child would probably do it.

He needed to get this over with. Quickly. He placed his hand over the microphone to prevent pickup. "If you want, I can read the name for you."

She set her chin and drew in a shaky breath, still not meeting his eyes. "I can do it."

He set the envelopes on the lectern. "Okay, the top envelope contains the recipient's name. Can you announce it and give the second envelope to the graduate?"

"I'd like to say a few words first."

He blinked. Apparently, she didn't own that determined chin for nothing. He lowered the microphone for her and moved out of her way. "Go for it."

She stepped forward, the crowd hushing to listen. "My sister would be so proud that every year a scholarship in her name will help students who love chemistry as much as she did."

Peter let out a fascinated breath. She was pulling herself together like a champ—without her twin's flare for drama, but with a vulnerability that tugged at him.

"Our family thanks Trenton Research Laboratories for their generous scholarship and Dr. Peter Sheridan for driving all the way from Madison to present it." Her soft voice ringing clear and unpretentious, she took the sheet of paper from the envelope, her face crumpling as she struggled with her emotions.

Tensing, Peter took a step toward her to help her out.

But a teary smile broke free. "I'm thrilled to announce the first recipient of the Clarissa Chandler Scholarship is Stacy Meyers."

The crowd erupted in a cheer. Several beach balls took to the humid air to be carried away by the breeze. Apparently, high school graduation in Noah's Crossing, Wisconsin was a different animal from the quiet ceremony that liberated him from boarding school twelve years ago.

The sturdy boy in Jessie's arms burrowed his face deeper into her neck.

Luckily, the kid seemed to be a resolute napper. Peter began to relax a little, the tension in his shoulders easing.

A tall, thin girl ran across the stage to the lectern, her face wreathed in smiles. She accepted the envelope from Jessie and hugged her without squashing the little guy in Jessie's arms.

"I'm so proud of you, Stacy." Jessie guided the excited teenager to the microphone, then stepped back alongside Peter.

Peter caught a breath of her scent. Fresh citrus. Very nice. He noted the same fair skin, patrician nose and high cheekbones as her twin, but Jessie let her hair hang free. Everything about her seemed gentler, warmer, less driven than her sister with the killer ambition and single-minded purpose. And Clarissa lovingly moving her hand over the child the way Jessie did? He couldn't imagine it.

Stacy Meyers held the envelope aloft to give everybody a good view. "I promise to work hard and make Jess and her family and everybody in Noah's Crossing proud of me." She gave Jessie another hug, shook Peter's hand as she thanked him, then ran off the stage and down the steps.

Peter finally breathed a relieved sigh. All was well that ended well, right? He'd done what he came to do and could soon get back to his research.

The little guy Jessie held shifted and turned his head, the breeze tousling his reddish-brown curls.

Jessie stroked his back. He was a cute kid.

Peter studied the baby's high forehead, his wide-set eyes, his prominent nose...and the small, diamond-shaped birthmark on the baby's lower left jaw.

A birthmark exactly like his own.

Hearing Dr. Sheridan murmur, Jessic looked into his frowning eyes. He stared at Jake as if he couldn't believe what he saw. A chill shaking her, her own focus snagged on the man's birthmark she'd been trying to ignore ever since walking on stage. The birthmark that was just like Jake's.

She swept her blowing hair away from her face with her free hand. Maybe she could believe the identical birthmarks were a coincidence if Jake wasn't the spitting image of the man—high forehead, rich auburn hair, deep brown eyes, right down to the cleft in his chin—or maybe if Clarissa hadn't worked at the Madison lab with Dr. Sheridan before she'd moved to the New York branch.

Dr. Sheridan turned his questioning gaze on her. "When this is over, we need to talk." His deep voice was a command.

Why would she want to talk to him? If he was Jake's father, what could she possibly have to say to the man her sister said was unavailable and completely uninterested in being a dad? With a shake of her head, she clutched Jake's warm, chubby body a little closer, turned and walked carefully down the stage steps, passed her father and sat down next to her mother. She stole a glance at Dr. Sheridan.

He'd taken his seat among the dignitaries on stage, his focus locked on Jake. The only word to describe the look on his face was shock.

Shock? What did *he* have to be shocked about? Shock was *her* thing.

Dad leaned to pat her arm. "You did us proud, Jess," he whispered.

Mom clasped Jessie's hand. "Are you all right?"

Jessie nodded vigorously to discourage conversation.

But Mom didn't let that stop her. She drew closer to whisper in Jessie's ear. "Jake looks just like him. What if…?"

"He wants to talk," Jessie whispered back.

Mom frowned.

Jessie glanced over her shoulder. Had friends and relatives filling the row behind her noticed how much Jake looked like Dr. Sheridan? It seemed impossible to miss.

Sighing, Mom settled back to listen to the program.

As if she would hear a word. Knowing Mom, she was busy putting the entire situation in God's hands.

Too bad Jessie couldn't. Not with her mind whirling with questions. If Dr. Sheridan was Jake's daddy, why hadn't he sent somebody else to present the scholarship? Was he curious to see his son? Had his "uninterested in being a dad" attitude changed?

A shiver snaking down her back, Jessie raised her gaze to the stage, past the valedictorian at the lectern to the magnetic, auburn-haired man sitting to the left. She shifted on the uncomfortable chair in an attempt to ease the pain in her hip. Why hadn't she insisted her sister tell her everything about Jake's father?

That was easy. She'd been so desperate to accept the wondrous gift her twin had offered, questions had been the last thing on her mind. Down deep, she hadn't wanted anything to get in the way of her raising Clarissa's beautiful baby boy.

She stroked Jake's back, her heart flooding with love and gratitude to the sister who'd given Jessie's life meaning when she'd thought it would never have meaning again. *I love you, Rissa. If Dr. Sheridan is Jake's daddy, you picked a man with great genes. But what does he think we need to talk about?*

Applause startled her as the valedictorian took his seat. Dr. Sheridan didn't seem to notice, absorbed in Jake as he was. People on stage took their places to hand out diplomas.

All Jessie could think about was the intensity on Dr. Sheridan's face when he'd said they needed to talk. Now, that potential conversation loomed so ominously, she had trouble breathing. What possible good could come from it?

Before she said one word to him, she needed to talk

to Will Kennedy. He was a lawyer. He could tell her if the adoption papers were in order and whether she might have anything to worry about if Dr. Sheridan really was Jake's daddy. She glanced at her watch. Will would be at the diner right about now for his daily piece of pie. If she hurried, she could catch him.

Red robes flapping in the wind, students began filing across the stage amid cheering and clapping and bouncing beach balls. Dr. Sheridan headed for the side stage steps.

Jessie grabbed her purse and turned to her parents. "I'm going to walk back to the diner."

Dad pointed at the cloudy sky. "You'd better ride with us."

"It's too far for you to carry Jake," Mom insisted, concern in her voice.

"I'll be fine," Jessie said impatiently. Would her parents ever stop treating her like a victim who needed to be coddled?

Adjusting her son in her arms, she stood and strode out of the stadium as if her life depended on how fast her gimpy leg would carry her.

Reaching the sidewalk, she heard Dr. Sheridan holler her name.

# Chapter Two

Heart pounding, Peter caught up with Jessie just as she swung around to face him, her hand flying to the little boy's head as if to protect him. Peter's blood pressure shot up a few more points. She, obviously, thought he was a threat.

He *was* acting a little crazy. The idea that this child could be his son *was* crazy. Clarissa would have told him she was pregnant after their night together, wouldn't she?

But if Jessie had nothing to hide, why did she run away? Did she think he wouldn't pursue her? That he wouldn't have to know? "Jessie, is this Clarissa's child?"

She took a step back.

Peter studied the baby's hair so much like Peter's mother's. The nose and chin cleft like his father's. "He looks like me. He even has the Sheridan birthmark."

Jessie stared at him as if he'd sprouted an extra eye in the middle of his forehead. "He's *my* son."

Peter stared her down. Shiny, luminous eyes...wide... with fear? Her breaths were fast and shallow. Her soft lips clenched tight as if guarding a secret.

He wanted to reassure her, tell her everything would be okay. Dragging a breath, he struggled to regain his focus.

The timing. Ever since he'd spotted the child's birthmark, his mind had been spinning to figure out the timing. If he was right, Clarissa would have been two months pregnant when she'd transferred to the New York lab. "He's about eighteen months old, isn't he?"

Jessie's eyes flinched.

Enough of a reaction to confirm he was right on the money.

Thunder rumbled low. He could smell the ozone in the air.

"I'm in a huge hurry." Jessie glanced away as if she couldn't wait to make a break for it. "I have to take care of something at my diner."

He shook his head. "Don't you think I have a right to know for sure that I have a son?"

She shuttered her gaze. "I…I don't have time to talk right now."

Attempting to tone down his frustration, he studied the lines puckering the creamy skin between her eyes. "I need to know if he's Clarissa's son. How much time can a simple yes or no take?"

Finally, she looked at him as if she'd made up her mind. "My diner's on Main Street. If you need to talk to me, stop in in a half hour or so." She turned, intent on leaving.

He couldn't let her go…not yet. Somehow, he had to make her trust him enough to give him an answer. "Jessie…if he is Clarissa's…"

Pausing, Jessie gave him a nervous glance.

Good. He had her attention. But if the baby was Clarissa's…what? He clenched his jaw. "I would have taken responsibility for him…if she'd told me she was pregnant."

Swinging around to face him, Jessie shot him a questioning scowl.

"She didn't tell me," he repeated.

The boy murmured.

Peter watched the child's tiny nose crinkle as if chasing a laugh in his dreams. Unexplainable warmth welled inside until he thought he'd choke on it. He reached to touch a chubby finger.

Jessie jerked out of his reach as if his touch would contaminate the kid.

Peter met her eyes. Sad eyes brimming with indescribable pain and fear. He felt like a heel for making her feel so threatened. But her actions gave him his answer. "The boy *is* Clarissa's. And mine."

She shifted her stance, biting her lip rather than confirming or rejecting his words.

Her silence was all the confirmation he needed.

"Mama?" The little guy raised his head and stretched, his back arching, his little butt jutting out.

"Hi, sweetheart," Jessie said softly. "You had a nice nap, didn't you?" Wary eyes on Peter, she kissed the baby's forehead.

The child gave her a smile that would make the sun seem dim in comparison. Then the boy turned his deep brown, Sheridan eyes on Peter.

A grin traveled through him like a beacon of light, and he wondered if the buttons on his shirt would pop with the pride swelling his chest. Odd, considering how little he'd had to do with the child's existence. "What's his name?"

"His name?" Jessie swallowed. "His name is Jacob Maxwell Chandler."

Peter couldn't miss the challenge in her tone. "An honorable name," he admitted. Too bad he'd had no part in choosing it. "Hi, Jacob."

The boy studied him almost as if sizing up their similarities.

Maybe Peter should introduce himself. Should he tell him he was his father? Maybe not. It was too soon for that. For the boy…for the woman holding him…and for himself. "My name is Peter."

"Pedo?"

"Close enough."

Another low rumble of thunder. Closer now.

"You need to understand how things are, Dr. Sheridan." Jessie's soft voice crackled with tension.

Peter raised his gaze from the child to meet her engaging eyes.

"I am Jake's mother." She straightened her shoulders. "Clarissa gave him to me before he was born. I was the first one to hold him, to give him a bath, to feed him. I'm the only mother he's known, and I couldn't love him more if I'd given him life."

Peter's jaw clenched. "She had no right to give him away."

Jessie's gaze darted to the ground as if she didn't want to see the truth, even with Peter standing right in front of her. Turning to face him, she lifted her chin. "He's *my* son. I adopted him. And I'll do whatever I have to do because there's no way I'll let you take him away from me. None." Chin high, she turned and limped away.

Throat tight, he watched her go, a mixture of feelings completely confusing him. She was so gentle and vulnerable…with a core of sheer determination. Hurting her was the last thing he wanted.

But it looked like he had a son he didn't know existed until now. Even if his life *was* his research. What in the world was he going to do with a kid?

He turned and strode for the parking lot, dodging a petite redhead who was jogging down the sidewalk in a dress and high heels. He'd better call his attorney and find out just what his rights and responsibilities were. Because before he met Jessie at the diner, he needed to gain some control of this situation.

Walking as fast as she could, Jessie glared straight ahead. *What is going on, God? You can't possibly expect me to give up Jake. Haven't I already lost enough?*

"Hey Jess, wait up."

"Maggie," Jake squealed.

Trying to rein in her panic without much success, Jessie turned.

"Hi, Jake." Her high-heeled best friend jogged to Jessie's side, barely out of breath. "You look even more upset than Dr. Sheridan does. What were you talking to that hunky man about?"

"That hunky man says he's Jake's father." Jessie had trouble recognizing the strained voice as her own.

"What?" Maggie turned to scowl at Dr. Sheridan's retreating physique. "Why would he say something like that?"

"You didn't notice how much they look alike?"

"Well, I suppose…but that doesn't mean…"

"He has the birthmark. He said it runs in his family. And he knows exactly how old Jake is."

Maggie looked confused. "He and Clarissa?"

"Apparently." Jessie swallowed hard. "She didn't tell him she was pregnant."

"What?" Maggie's big brown eyes rolled. "What was she thinking?"

"He says she had no right to give him to—" Her voice broke.

"Now calm down, Jess." Maggie threw her hands in the air like she always did when she was upset. "Let's just think a minute. First, he hasn't taken a paternity test, so we don't know he's the daddy. And second, if he is, you have the adoption papers, right?"

Jessie nodded, afraid to trust her voice.

Maggie's hands darted dramatically. "We both know Clarissa was a stickler for making sure everything was very legal and in order. So even if he does turn out to be Jake's dad, what can he do about it?"

Jessie wanted to believe Maggie's words, but...

"Nada," Maggie said as if the whole matter was settled. "Wait here while I get my car."

Jessie's head spun. She needed time to calm down and get her defenses back in place. "Walking is my physical therapy, remember?"

"But it's going to rain." Maggie pointed at the sky. "Besides, Jake is too heavy."

"Maggie...." Jessie had warned her friend to quit treating her like she needed help or she'd have to look for a new best friend. Maggie had agreed to watch it, but she still needed reminding.

"Fine." Maggie narrowed her eyes. "You sure you're okay?"

"I'm perfect," Jessie snapped. She didn't even want to think about how protective Maggie and her parents would be if they knew the accident had left her with injuries less obvious than her limp...injuries nothing could ever heal.

* * *

Rain was starting, Jake felt like he weighed a hundred pounds and Jessie's hip was killing her by the time she struggled up the diner steps. She hoped Will was still inside.

Jake's adoption had to hold up in court. Like Maggie said, Clarissa had always been thorough, and she would have made certain the father-not-knowing-about-the-baby loophole was closed. Wouldn't she?

She pulled open the door, the bell above it jingling to announce them. The interior's cool, dry air confirmed her new AC was doing its job. Her cousin Lisa, who was behind the counter, and several customers sitting on Jessie's new, red vinyl stools greeted them. Jake returned their greetings by opening and closing both little fists in his rendition of a wave.

With a sigh of relief, Jessie spotted Will, the upperclassman who'd gone to college on a basketball scholarship and returned to Noah's Crossing with a law degree not long after her accident. She'd still been in physical therapy when he'd asked her out on a pity date, probably engineered by Aunt Lou. At least Aunt Lou tried to organize everybody's lives, not just Jessie's.

But her refusal to date Will didn't mean they weren't still friends. It didn't keep him from stopping in the diner for pie almost every afternoon, either. "Hey, Will. Can I have a word with you in the back room?"

The corners of Will's sharp blue eyes wrinkled. "Right now?"

Jessie noticed the fork in his hand and the half-eaten pie à la mode on the plate in front of him. "Bring your pie with you. You want a cup of coffee on the house?"

"Can't pass that up, now, can I?" His puzzled look intact, Will stood to tower over the counter.

Actually, Will wasn't any taller than Dr. Sheridan, was he? Jessie pushed the image of the handsome, authoritative doctor from her mind and strode for the curtain that separated the customer area from the prep-and-storage room. She needed to focus.

Lisa poured Will's cup of coffee. "You look upset."

Jessie met her eyes. "I'm fine," she said automatically.

"Well, you don't look fine." Lisa handed the steaming coffee to Will.

"Thanks," he said.

Jessie ducked through the curtain and headed for the play corner she'd fenced off near one of the long windows. "Look, Jake. There's Thomas the engine, right where you left him."

"Tomut!" Jake threw himself with glee, totally oblivious to the concept of gravity.

But Jessie was ready for his lunge and stopped him from falling. She hoped he outgrew his habit before he got much heavier and harder to contain. "Slow down, okay?"

Jake touched her cheek in the sweet apology that always melted her heart. Then he turned, wriggling for release.

She bent over the mesh fence to set him down, pain stabbing her hip and making her catch her breath. "There you go."

"There you goes," he mimicked, scurrying to his low train table.

Will chuckled. "He's talking more every day." Setting his empty plate near the sink, he leaned against the counter. "How'd you hurt your leg?"

Jessie frowned. "My leg is fine."

Will took a sip of coffee and wisely decided to change

the subject. "You outdid yourself with that raspberry-rhubarb pie. I think it's my new favorite." He gave her a little grin.

She attempted a smile, then gave it up as she hurried to the fireproof safe where she kept her important papers. Grasping her ring of keys from her purse, she knelt and unlocked the box. She clasped the folder marked "Jake," struggled to her feet and handed it to Will.

He looked at the identifying tab, then at Jessie. "Jake?"

"Clarissa hired a lawyer she knew in New York to handle the legal work for the private adoption. I'm sure everything is as it should be, but will you look at it to make sure?"

"Any reason for your sudden interest?"

She squinted. "It seems I met Jake's father today. He made the scholarship presentation at graduation. He says Clarissa didn't tell him about Jake." Her words sounded clipped, almost matter-of-fact, but the breathless panic ringing in her ears told the real story.

Will set his cup beside his pie plate, bent his head and thumbed through the contents of the folder.

Hanging on to a calm she didn't feel, Jessie tried to read Will's face as he studied Jake's birth certificate and papers documenting the adoption. "We dotted every i and crossed every t, didn't we?"

Will looked up. "The documents that are here look perfect."

She wanted to heave a sigh of relief, but his serious tone warned her there was more.

"In Wisconsin, a single mother doesn't need to identify the father on the baby's birth certificate, but if Clarissa didn't tell him she was pregnant, and his DNA proves he's the father, he has a legitimate claim."

Jessie stared in horror. "How much of a claim?"

"He'd need a court order, but if he has the means to care for Jake, a judge could very well award him at least partial custody."

"No," she heard herself moan, pain wrenching deep inside.

"I'm really sorry, Jess. Why didn't Clarissa tell him?"

"She said he was completely uninterested in being a father. I had no idea she hadn't told him. She wouldn't even tell me who the father was." A thought nudged Jessie's mind. Had her sister wanted to give Jessie her dream of being a mother so much that she'd convinced herself the father wouldn't care? If Dr. Sheridan hadn't come to Noah's Crossing to present the scholarship, Jake's father's would still be a mystery.

"Look—even if he proves to be Jake's father, are you sure he wants custody?" Will asked.

Jessie thought about the look on Dr. Sheridan's face when he'd reached out to touch Jake. About the intensity in his tone when he'd insisted Clarissa had no right to give Jake away. She swiped at tears clouding her vision. "I don't know. But he can't have Jake. You have to help me. I'll do whatever I need to do."

"Are you convinced the guy is Jake's dad?"

She'd give anything to be able to say no. Promise anything if God would just make the man go away like none of this was happening. But she knew things didn't work that way. "Yes. I believe he is Jake's father."

"Then try to find a compromise to keep him from taking you to court."

"Compromise?" She shook her head. "I'll never compromise where Jake is concerned."

"Wouldn't a compromise be better than losing him?"

She drew a sharp breath.

"It could happen, Jess."

"Doesn't it matter that Jake's mother didn't want the father to know? That she wanted *me* to raise him?"

"It's a factor in your favor. So are the adoption papers. But…I know Jake means the world to you. I don't advise you to risk it." Will handed the file folder to her. "Is the guy married?"

"I don't think so. He doesn't wear a ring anyway."

"Does he know anything about raising kids?"

"I don't know that, either." She put the folder back in the safe, fumbled to lock it, then dropped her keys in her purse.

Will rubbed the back of his neck. "The thought of being a single dad would scare me to death. Watching all you do with Jake, I can see I wouldn't know the first thing about how to take care of a kid."

Her mind seized on Will's words. If Dr. Sheridan was single…did he know what being a single father would involve? If he knew, would he be afraid of taking it on like Will was?

"Jess." Lisa held the curtain divider aside. "I'm sorry to interrupt, but a tall, good-looking guy in a suit insists on seeing you. And he's not a patient man."

# Chapter Three

Feeling more in charge of things, Peter brushed rain off his shoulders, the succulent aroma of roasting meat and mouth-watering sweets in Jessie's Main Street Diner reminding him he hadn't eaten lunch. He ignored the din of diners eating at the busy counter and gave a curt nod to the tall, unfriendly looking guy emerging through the colorful curtain, cup of coffee in hand. A relative? A boyfriend? Was Jessie circling the wagons already?

Well, gentle and vulnerable or not, let her try to stop him from seeing his son and he'd straighten her out in a hurry. He'd called his attorney, who had assured him that he did, indeed, have responsibilities and rights if he was the boy's father, and his rights could even trump hers in a court of law if Peter decided to take it that far.

Strange. He was too absorbed in his research to think he'd ever get married, let alone have a kid. Finding out he *had* one was shocking, amazing and overwhelming. But he had to admit, the idea was beginning to grow on him.

Deep inside, he was convinced the boy was his. But that hadn't stopped him from picking up DNA kits at the local drugstore. A few quick cheek swabs would prevent future questions…his or anybody else's.

Clutching the drugstore bag, he ducked into the back room. His glance took in stoves, refrigerators and a huge sink. A long counter held baking paraphernalia, and shelves stacked with boxes lined one wall.

Jessie stood in the middle of the room, her blue eyes snapping with challenge, her slender body tense and skittish as a filly about to bolt.

He had the unmistakable urge to gentle her. A pretty outrageous thought from a guy who'd never had time for a serious relationship.

"Pedo."

Peter grinned, amazed the little fella remembered his name. His gaze swept to the boy standing at a low table in a fenced-off corner filled with toys. The toddler was dwarfed by a mural on the wall above him of a blue train with an impish smile. "How's it going, Jacob?"

The little guy pointed to himself. "Jake."

"Jake? Then Jake it is."

"Tomut." The boy held up a small toy for Peter to admire.

Peter took a step closer.

Jessie shot between them, eyes flashing. "What do you want?" She stared at the bag in his hand.

He raked his hand through his thick, short hair and decided to lay it on the line. "I need a cheek swab from each of you for DNA testing."

"DNA testing?"

"You and Clarissa were identical twins, so you have the same DNA. A sample from you will strengthen the DNA test probabilities."

She shook her head. "I need to talk to my lawyer before I agree to that."

He frowned. "I think we both know a DNA test is just a formality. But it will clear up lingering doubts. I'd like to take samples back to Madison with me. Will you call your lawyer? I need to get on the road soon."

She chewed her pretty bottom lip.

"I phoned my attorney," he said. "He told me I have a legal right to my son."

She shot him a scowl. "Do you know *anything* about kids?"

Absolutely nothing. But… "I'm a quick study."

"I'll take that to mean you don't know about kids or the practicalities of having a toddler in your life."

He rubbed his forehead, which had begun to throb. "Jessie…I'm still getting used to the fact that my son exists. Practicalities might take me a little while."

She narrowed her eyes. "Is sarcasm the best you can do, Dr. Sheridan?"

"Sorry. I've been caught a little off guard here."

"And I haven't?" She blew out an impatient breath.

"Pedo." Jake held up the toy again.

Jessie turned to the little guy. "Mommy's talking to Peter right now, sweetheart."

"No." Jake shook his head. "Pedo. Tomut."

Giving Peter a warning look, she stepped aside.

Peter strode over and squatted to peer at the blue engine Jake held in his chubby fist. "Nice train." He pointed at the mural. "Just like the picture."

"Tomut."

Peter looked up to Jessie. "I think we need an interpreter."

She swallowed as if forcing down a bitter pill. "He's saying Thomas—the name of his favorite engine."

"Thank you." He tried to smile. No doubt coming face to face with Jake's dad had to be a shock for her.

Maybe as much of a shock as Peter finding out he had a son.

Jake reached out and fingered the colorful tie hanging loosely around Peter's neck. "Putty?"

"Putty," Peter agreed, whatever it meant.

"He thinks your tie is pretty," Jessie offered.

"Oh…pretty." Peter glanced over his shoulder at her. "Thank you."

"Nana? Weesa?"

Peter squinted, unable to decipher who or what Nana and Weesa were.

"Nana is his gramma and Lisa is the woman behind the counter out front," Jessie explained. "He's asking where they are."

Jake looked from Jessie back to Peter and broke into a big grin.

Peter laughed, the sound unfamiliar to his ears. "You know we're talking about you, don't you?"

Giggling, Jake whirled, toddled over to the low table and began pushing his engine around the track, chattering away in a dialect that had no resemblance to language as Peter knew it.

It appeared the boy's curiosity about Peter had been satisfied. Peter stood and turned to Jessie. "He's an alert, intelligent little boy. Obviously, you're doing an amazing job with him."

"Thank you." She frowned as if unsure she could trust his sincerity. "I don't want him to hear us." She walked across the room.

Peter followed her.

She stopped and turned to him. "Clarissa said Jake's father was unavailable and had no interest in being a father."

A little too close to the truth?

"Are you married?" she asked.

He almost laughed. When would he have time to get married? "Clarissa and I spent one night together. I'm too dedicated to my research to have time for relationships. Clarissa knew that. Maybe that's what she meant."

"Too dedicated to be a father? That's the way she felt about being a mother." Jessie's sad eyes told him she'd never understand her sister's decision.

"So she left the baby with you and your parents to raise and went back to New York as if he didn't exist?"

Jessie shook her head. "She never pretended he didn't exist. You're not being fair."

"*I'm* not being fair? Clarissa wasn't fair to any of us."

"Not fair?" Jessie's blue eyes narrowed. "She gave me the most precious gift she could have given me."

Peter opened his mouth to remind her Clarissa had no right to give the baby away. But Jessie's vulnerable admission struck an empathetic chord inside him, and he swallowed his words.

Jessie let out a breath. "Do you have family?"

"Family? Why?"

"What's going on here?" The woman in the graduation audience he'd identified as Mrs. Chandler hustled into the room.

"Nana!" Jake squealed, pointing with delight.

She strode over to the boy, bent and gave him a hug, then turned to Jessie. "Are you all right?"

"Yes," Jessie answered curtly.

Peter blinked. Jessie wasn't even fooling him that she was all right. Did she think she could fool her mother?

Apparently not. Like a mother bear protecting her young, Mrs. Chandler focused distrusting blue eyes on Peter. "Why are you here?"

Even with disapproval written on the older woman's face, there was no question where her daughters had gotten their Nordic beauty. "I'm sorry to upset you, Mrs. Chandler. I came to Noah's Crossing to honor Clarissa and to express my deep sympathy to you and your family."

"Thank you." Mrs. Chandler's hand fluttered to her throat, but her direct gaze didn't falter. "Are you his father?"

"Yes, I believe I am."

Shaking her head as if she had trouble believing him, Mrs. Chandler turned and walked to the stove. She jerked open the oven door and set a big pan on the counter with a thud. "Where were you when Clarissa needed you?"

Might just as well be blunt. "She didn't tell me she was pregnant."

"What?" Mrs. Chandler's head shot up.

"I didn't know."

She glared at him as if she could see straight through him. "Dear Father in heaven…" Her lips continuing to move, she bent her head over her work, lifted a huge hunk of meat from the pan to a cutting board, slid a knife from a large holder on the counter and began slicing.

Peter had never seen anybody wield a knife so fast. In light of her obvious distrust, he was relieved she was carving the meat and not him.

The thunk of the knife pausing, Mrs. Chandler nailed him with her gaze. "Why would she not tell you she was pregnant?"

He wouldn't allow his gaze to shift away. "Well… she knew I'm dedicated to my work."

Mrs. Chandler heaved a heavy sigh. "Sounds familiar." Her tone one of resignation, she began slicing meat at the speed of sound again, as if the practical task helped her make sense of things. "You two must have made quite a couple."

"We weren't a couple," he clarified.

Both women's questioning gazes flew to his face.

"What I mean is…we…were together only once. I… don't have time for anything but my work." Face hot, he shut his eyes. And his mouth. There was no way out of the hole he'd dug himself into. He sounded like he'd used and abandoned the daughter and sister these women loved. Only he and Clarissa knew what happened, and no way was he going to try to explain the situation to her mother and sister.

Mrs. Chandler tore a piece of tinfoil off a roll and began wrapping meat in it. "Just what do you want, Dr. Sheridan? What are you doing here?"

"He wants DNA samples from Jake and me," Jessie explained.

Mrs. Chandler narrowed her eyes. "If you're so sure you're his father, why do you need a DNA test? For legal reasons?"

"DNA confirmation will clear up any questions."

"Don't let him have samples, Jess. Not without talking to a lawyer first."

"I won't. Did you drop Dad off at home?"

"Yes." Mrs. Chandler exchanged a look with Jessie. Unfortunately, Peter couldn't read it.

"I parked the van right out front," Mrs. Chandler said.

Jessie walked over and lifted Jake out of his play area

as if she had a plan. "Let's take your musical car with us, okay?"

"Yay." Jake clapped his hands.

"Are you planning to talk to a lawyer?" Peter asked.

"Yes."

"Great. I'll follow you. It will save time so I can get on the road sooner."

"Leave Jake with me." Mrs. Chandler gave Peter a worried look, clearly wanting to keep him as far away from his son as she could.

"Mom, you and Lisa will have your hands full with the after-graduation crowd. Uncle Harold and Aunt Lou aren't coming in until later to help with the supper rush."

The diner sounded like a family affair. Jessie must have a whole army of relatives. After this run-in with her mother, he sure wasn't eager to meet her extended family.

Jessie strode past Peter. "You can ride with us."

He'd feel more in control if he drove. "We can take my car."

"No. Jake's car seat is in the van," Jessie said.

Car seat? He'd heard women in the lab discussing which kind was safest. He'd have to do some research before he bought one for his own car. *Whoa, aren't you getting a little ahead of yourself, Sheridan?*

Mrs. Chandler handed a small package of foil-wrapped meat to Jessie. "Take this home with you."

Home? Had Peter missed something? He needed to get things straight. "After we stop at the lawyer's, you will bring me back to pick up my car before you go home, right?"

"We're not stopping at the lawyer's." She gave him a sober look. "I'm taking you home to meet my dad."

Was she kidding? Why would he want to meet her dad? "Some other time, maybe. It's important I get the cheek swabs ASAP and start the drive back. I have work waiting for me at the lab."

Jessie narrowed her eyes. "While you talk to my dad, I will call my lawyer."

Peter saw flint in her beautiful, crystal-blue gaze. Clearly, she was giving him an ultimatum with no room for compromise. He reached to massage his stiff neck.

"While you're home, Jess, put your feet up for a while," her mother directed.

"I won't have time, Mother," Jessie answered tensely. "I'll be back by five. Please call if you need me before then." Frowning, she disappeared through the curtain dividing the room from the customer area.

Peter stared after her. Why couldn't she call her lawyer from the diner? And why did she insist he talk to her father?

"You'd better catch her if you want a chance at that DNA sample, Dr. Sheridan," her mother prodded.

Jessie climbed into the van out of the rain, started the motor and pulled away from the curb, back stiff, white-knuckle grip on the wheel. The windshield wipers clacking back and forth irritated her frayed nerves. But they didn't hold a candle to the passenger beside her. At least his subtly spicy aftershave wasn't as overpowering in the intimate space as the man himself was.

The idea of taking him home for a talk with Dad had come to her straight out of the blue. If anybody could make Dr. Sheridan think twice before he leapt into uncharted waters, Dad could. Hadn't he saved her from making bad decisions more than once?

She'd much rather let Dr. Sheridan follow her in the nifty little sports car he'd pointed out to Jake when they got in the van. But insisting he ride with them was the only way to find out all she could about him and his support system. Because if she, indeed, did have to find a way to compromise as Will advised, she wanted to know just how much.

Looking every bit as uncomfortable as Jessie felt, Dr. Sheridan shifted to peer at Jake in his car seat in the back.

"Car," Jake squealed.

Dr. Sheridan laughed awkwardly. "I hear it, loud and clear."

Jessie glanced in the rearview mirror at Jake holding his musical car out to be admired, then turned her attention to her passenger. "I suppose your parents will be glad to hear they have a grandson." Her voice sounded shrill when she'd only meant to raise it to allow him to hear her over the tinny tune of Jake's car.

"I think they'll be happy the Sheridan genes will survive another generation," he said dryly.

She gave him a serious frown. "You don't sound as if you know them very well."

The drugstore bag crackled in his long fingers, his silence answering her.

She pulled to a stop at the intersection and returned waves from people walking home from graduation, umbrellas raised against the rain. She turned to Dr. Sheridan. "Why don't you know your parents?"

He gave her a sideways glance. "They're archeologists. They spend most of their time on digs in remote parts of the world."

"Interesting." And a relief. It didn't sound like he'd get much help or support from them, did it? She accelerated.

He stretched his long legs out in front of him until he ran out of room.

She jerked her gaze back to the road in front of them.

"Any chance Jake's car has a volume control?" he asked. "Those nonsensical rhymes just began a painful third rotation."

Were the good doctor's nerves a tad on the frazzled side, too? *And* unused to children's toys? "I don't want him to hear the tension in our voices."

"I didn't think of that."

"You would have if you knew anything about kids."

His lips quirked. "No doubt."

She drew in a momentary breath of victory. But it was too soon to gloat. She still didn't know much about his situation or who he depended on for support. "Did you travel with your parents when you were young?"

"No."

Her little fishing expedition would take forever if all she got from him were one-syllable answers. Drawing herself a little taller, she took a left and fired off another question. "Who did you stay with?"

"I lived in boarding schools," he said matter-of-factly.

She looked at him sharply. Boarding schools? The poor man. "You grew up in boarding schools?" She couldn't keep the shock out of her voice.

He stared out the windshield. "The best boarding schools in the country."

As if that made it easier for him to be away from his family? "Did your parents *sometimes* take you with them?"

He glanced her way. "Why the third degree?"

She recognized avoidance when she heard it. "Did they?"

He dragged in a breath and let it out. "There's not much for a kid to do in the middle of the Sahara desert for months on end. And they wanted me educated by the best schools available to better prepare me to contribute to mankind."

His parents sacrificed him to science? How could they do that? "You must have been lonely growing up with strangers."

He shrugged as if loneliness was no big deal. "My studies were challenging. There was plenty to do. Swimming, tennis, golf, horses, you name it. I didn't have time to be lonely."

He expected her to believe that? "Did you go home often?"

He frowned at her.

"Did you?" She sat straighter. "Go home often?"

"When holidays didn't conflict with digs." His tone was flat, uninterested.

Jessie swallowed, unable to comprehend the lonely, disconnected childhood he must have lived. "What about when you were very little? Before boarding school?"

"I had nannies."

Jessie shook her head. How did a child function and grow without his parents and relatives to guide him? How did he learn to love himself or others if he didn't have people who loved him show him how? How would he love Jake? "I have a hard time imagining growing up like that. I'm related to half of Noah's Crossing."

"Lucky you."

She glanced at his serious face and somehow wanted

to make him feel better. "I'm sure you've made your parents proud."

"Yes," he said quietly.

Too quietly. He'd had such a lonely, awful childhood, Jessie's heart ached for him. But was his childhood the reason he wanted his son? Even if he had no time for him?

He didn't have a wife. No girlfriend either if he'd been honest about not having time for relationships. But he must have somebody besides his absent parents. Somebody he was counting on for help. "You said you don't have time for relationships, but you must have *somebody*."

He raised a well-shaped eyebrow. "Why are you so interested?"

"Because of Jake, of course."

"You need somebody to vouch that I won't be a bad influence on the boy? Is that it?"

"Do you have anybody who would do that?"

Jaw clenching, he settled back in his seat and focused out the windshield again. "Scott and Karen Kenyon."

"Friends?"

"He was my college professor and has been my friend and mentor ever since. Is that a long enough relationship for you?" He sounded a tad irritated.

Maybe she was finally getting somewhere. "Have you called to tell them about Jake?"

"Not yet."

"Do they have children?"

"They'd make great parents, but kids aren't in the cards for them," he said sadly.

She couldn't help empathizing with them. But a jolt of fear chased away her empathy. Did he want his friends to raise Jake? "They can't have children?"

"They have enough on their plates without kids to worry about."

This wasn't adding up. If his friends didn't have time for children, he couldn't count on them to help him with Jake, could he? "I don't understand."

He rubbed his chin. "Scott was diagnosed with ALS—you probably know it as Lou Gehrig's disease—almost two years ago."

"I'm sorry."

"Neurological diseases are my specialty." He crumpled the bag in his hands. "I never dreamed the battle would become personal." No mistaking the passion in his voice now.

How could she not admire his dedication to his friend? She couldn't imagine the pressure he must feel to save him. "How is he doing?"

"The disease is taking its toll. But we've developed a promising experimental drug. We're hoping it will help Scott."

She glanced at him. "I'll pray for you and your friend."

His eyes rounded, then narrowed as if he didn't know how to respond.

"You don't believe in prayer?" she asked.

He dropped his gaze. "I believe in research."

Jessie focused on the wet road again. "It seems to me research and prayer would go hand in hand."

"Why do you say that?"

"Well, you're looking for answers to heal people. Who better to ask for help than the Great Healer?" She could feel him studying her.

"I never thought about it that way," he said.

She wanted to tell him maybe he should. After all,

the idea of life without prayer was as foreign to her as life without family.

"Does God hear your prayers, Jessie?" he asked softly.

She bit her lip. "I honestly don't know anymore." Because if He did, Peter Sheridan wouldn't be here threatening to take Jake away.

# Chapter Four

The rain had stopped by the time Peter peered uneasily up the gravel drive to the small Cape Cod where Jessie's dad waited. Fumbling to unhook his seatbelt, he turned to watch Jessie make a game of unfastening Jake from his car seat, her movements gentle and caring. In spite of her distrust of Peter, there was such a warmth about her, especially when she interacted with Jake.

Could he ever be the kind of parent who showed his son he cared with every move? Given his lack of a role model, he didn't know where to begin. He didn't even know if he had it in him to love his son.

Jessie's questions about his family, or lack of one, were legitimate concerns. If Scott and Karen hadn't taken him under their protective wings in college, he'd have no one. With his lack in the relationship department, how would he be able to relate to a little boy?

Then there was his research, a demanding taskmaster that took everything he had to give. He lived it, breathed it. He'd focused on ALS research as a result of Scott's diagnosis. And as Scott's condition worsened, too many nights Peter slept on the cot in his office rather than making the drive downtown to his dingy, furnished apartment. Even when he had to be away from the lab, he was thinking, planning, solving problems related to his research.

Fine by him. Without his dedication, the experimental drug wouldn't be ready for testing. The drug that could be Scott's last chance.

Drugstore bag in hand, he climbed out of the van.

Jessie lifted Jake out of his seat and pushed the door shut. "You ready to meet my dad, Dr. Sheridan?"

"Sure." A lie. He doubted her father would take too kindly to the man who got his daughter pregnant and hadn't taken responsibility for her or the baby. Never mind that she hadn't bothered to tell him. Maybe Peter could hold his own with that fact. "Please call me Peter."

"Peter," she repeated, as if trying it out.

He liked the way his name sounded coming from her lips. "What's your father like?"

"He's a straight shooter. Protective. A great dad. And he loves Jake."

Peter heard love and pride in her voice, along with challenge. "Glad you're not in my shoes?"

She shot him a look that might pass for sympathetic.

Oh well. If talking to her father was the price to pay for a couple cheek swabs, bring him on. With fresh rain making the earth smell new again, Peter followed Jessie up the driveway into a backyard exuberant with flowering bushes and plants. A child's swing set filled the corner under a tree. The whine of a small motor came from a covered patio running the length of the house and outfitted as an outdoor living area. A muscular, weathered man sat at a workbench, using an electric sander on a long board. Had to be Jessie's father. "Your dad looks busy."

"He builds custom furniture in his free time. He has a shop in the garage."

"Papa!" Jake squealed.

Mr. Chandler switched off the sander and rose to Peter's height. "Hey, Jake. How you doing, little buddy?"

Jessie walked over to her dad.

Mr. Chandler bent and gave her a kiss on the forehead. "Your mother called. Said you were on your way."

The understanding passing between father and daughter hit Peter like a blow. So much said with just a look. The same understanding Jessie and her mother had shared. Communication real families enjoyed. He couldn't imagine communicating with his son like that.

Mr. Chandler reached across his workbench to give Peter's hand a firm shake. "Dr. Sheridan."

"Peter."

"Max."

"I want you to know how sorry I am about Clarissa's death."

"Thank you." The older man shifted his gaze to the ground as if checking his emotions. Then he raised his eyes, held out his arms and Jake lunged from Jessie's arms to his. "How's my little buddy?"

Jake gave his grandpa an enthusiastic hug.

Peter found himself smiling at the comradery between the two. It was hard not to smile at just about everything about the little guy.

"Come on, Jake." Jessie held up the tinfoil package

her mother had sent with her. "Help me put supper in the oven to stay warm, okay?"

"'Kay!" Jake yelled as if Jessie had given him a very important assignment.

Max let him slide to the ground.

Jessie grasped the boy's hand.

With a purposeful strut, Jake headed for the house with Jessie gliding beside him.

She was probably leaving so her father wouldn't have to pull punches. "You will make that phone call?" Peter reminded.

"I will," she called over her shoulder.

Peter dragged his gaze back to the man on the other side of the work bench.

Her father's eyes bore into Peter's until the screen door slammed behind Jessie and Jake. "My wife and I are very proud of both our daughters. But for reasons I'll never understand, Clarissa felt her research was more important than being a mother. What I want to know is why she found it necessary to keep her baby a secret from you."

Off and running. "I don't know the answer to that question."

Max studied Peter, sadness filling his lined face.

It must be hard to lose a child.

"I could use something cool." Max strode to the back wall. He pulled a couple cans from an under-counter refrigerator, strode back to Peter and handed him a can of Dr Pepper.

"Thanks." Peter popped the lid, the hiss of carbonated air filling the silence between them.

Max raised his soda. "To reasonable men."

Peter could hope. But the steel glint in Max's eyes warned him to stay on his toes. He raised his can in a toast, then took a sizable swallow, the liquid cold and refreshing.

Max drank thirstily before he lowered his can and focused a narrow gaze on Peter. "Clarissa and I had our differences of opinion, but she knew what she was doing when she gave Jake to Jessie. Jessie's the best thing that could have happened to that boy."

Peter had no argument with that. Just thinking about the love on her face when she looked at Jake made him smile. "She's wonderful with him."

"Think about it, Peter. If Clarissa had been a different person, she might have given him to some agency for adoption. You would never have known you had a son. And little Jake would have been lost to all of us."

Peter could only stare at the man as he absorbed his words. Rather than blaming Clarissa for leaving him out of the loop, maybe he should be thankful for the things she'd done right. He could only imagine how difficult the situation had been for her.

But Max wasn't finished. "The way I see it…the measure of a man is in how he takes care of his family. If you're the man I hope you are, you'll do what's best for Jake. If you don't, you don't deserve to be his father."

Somehow Max had managed to challenge Peter's integrity, prod him to live up to it and shame him if he fell short. The man was good. "Of course, I want what's best for Jake."

Max took a drink of his soda. "What's best for Jake is Jessie."

As if summoned, she walked out of the house, Jake in her arms. "Jake left his musical car out here."

She was just as pretty in jeans and a green T-shirt as she'd been in her sundress, Peter noted.

"Want a Dr Pepper, Jess?" Her father looked at her expectantly.

She shook her head.

"Did you talk to your lawyer?"

"Yes. He said I'll have to give you DNA samples eventually anyway, and I'd just as soon do it now."

"Great. Then let's get started." Peter swept the kits out of the drugstore bag he carried.

Max gave him a level gaze. "There's more to being a father than DNA, Peter."

"Of course there is."

"Like feelings, love, commitment. How do you feel about being a father?" Max asked.

Peter laid the kits on the nearby table. "Jake's great."

"Yes, he is. But that's not my question."

He should have known Jessie's dad wouldn't accept a superficial answer. Buying time, he laid out vials, small packages of swabs and labels while he sorted through thoughts he'd been struggling with about what to do regarding his son.

Bottom line? No way could he let Jake grow up without a father, like Peter had. "Jake needs to know his father. I can't let him grow up thinking he doesn't matter to me."

"Fair enough. But think long and hard about how best to accomplish that. As long as you remember what's best for him, we'll get along just fine."

In other words, as long as he remembered Jessie was best for Jake, everything would go smoothly. A not-too-veiled threat if Peter ever heard one. But he admired Jessie's father for laying it on the line.

Max looked at Peter, obviously waiting for him to be just as straightforward about what he wanted.

Peter's thoughts began to gain clarity. He wanted more than just to know his son and his son to know him. He wanted the kind of relationship with Jake that Jessie and her dad had.

And if that was what he wanted, he needed to step up to the plate. "Jessie's fortunate to have you, Max. You're here when she needs you, and you're not afraid to go to bat for her. I don't want to be anything less for my son."

"What?" Jessie's eyes went wide. "You want to be a father like my dad? But you have to get back to your lab, remember?"

She was right. He'd been in a hurry to get the DNA swabs so he could get on the road. Slight change of plans. If he was going to be a real father, he needed to get to know his son a little better. "I've decided to stay in town the rest of the weekend."

Unfortunately, the shock on Jessie's face wasn't the least bit encouraging.

In the steamy little bathroom, Jake's shampoo mingled with the subtle spice of Peter Sheridan's aftershave.

"Make bubbos," Jake squealed, slapping the water in the tub with both hands.

Jessie rocked back on her haunches to duck a spray of soapy water, a jab in her hip making her wince.

On his knees beside her, Peter took the splash at full force. Laughing, he swiped his hand over his wet face, his arm bumping Jessie's.

He turned to her, his laughing brown eyes concerned. "Sorry. You okay?"

She nodded vigorously, his presence seeming to fill the room.

His gaze softened. "I tend to throw myself into things, I'm afraid."

She squinted. Too warm, she scooched over to allow him more space.

"Pedo. Chug."

With an apologetic little smile, Peter turned to Jake and went back to making chugging noises and pushing a plastic tugboat in circles while Jake laughed and clapped and wildly slapped the water.

Grateful that Peter's focus was back on Jake, Jessie gave her head a little shake. What was her problem? Did she need to remind herself of Peter's declaration in the backyard this afternoon? He seemed to think he could pull Dad's qualities out of thin air. Ha.

She had to make him see reality. That's why she'd invited him to help with Jake's bath and bedtime ritual— to give him a glimpse of real-life, behind-the-scenes parenting. If he understood being a parent was time-consuming, sometimes heart-wrenching and a lot of hard work, he'd have to understand he lacked the time and the skills to care for Jake.

At first, Peter sat back and watched her play quietly with her son to calm him down before bed. But it hadn't taken him long to roll up his sleeves and take charge. Now, the front of his white dress shirt was soaked, and his black suit pants weren't faring much better. But he seemed oblivious to everything except Jake and how much fun they were having.

But right before bed? Not a good idea. The more tired Jake got, the more wound up he became, and the harder it would be to get him to settle down for the night.

Of course, it would give Peter a good dose of one of the challenges of parenting. He needed to get a complete picture. And as much as she didn't want Jake having a hard time settling down, maybe it would be worth it if Peter could see he wasn't up to the job. Struggling to her feet, she grabbed a dry towel and glanced pointedly at her watch. "Jake's bedtime has come and gone."

"Hear that, Jake? Time for bed."

Jake splashed, water flying. "Pedo chug."

Diversion worked better than going the direct route, but Peter would find that out soon enough. She gave him the towel.

"Thanks. Come on Jake, let's get you dried off."

Jake stuck out his bottom lip in his mutiny pose.

Peter looked up at her, amusement crinkling his rich brown eyes. To his credit, he didn't laugh even if Jake's pout *was* the cutest thing in the entire world.

Jake slapped the water, sending it flying everywhere again. "Chug, Pedo."

Peter turned back to Jake, a broad grin on his lips, as if that would help. He held the towel at the ready like he expected Jake to walk right into it. "See? Jessie gave me a big, fluffy towel to dry you off."

Jake pointed to Jessie. "Mama."

She smiled.

"Mama," Peter conceded.

"Chug, Pedo." Jake grasped the tugboat and jammed it at Peter.

Peter shook his head. "No more chugging. The tugboat's tired. It needs to go to bed."

Nice try.

But Jake was beyond listening. He flipped onto his tummy in the water, pushing the tugboat and making his motor sound.

Peter turned to Jessie. "Feel free to step in any time."

"But you're doing so well."

"You're enjoying this, aren't you?"

"Of course not," she fibbed.

"Any suggestions?"

"Well…" Maybe she should give him a crumb. "You could offer him his bedtime snack."

He gave an aha nod and turned to Jake. "How about a snack, Jake?"

Jake kept pushing the boat and making the chugging noise, totally absorbed in his imaginary world.

"Hey, Jake. What do you like for your snack?" Peter tried again. When Jake ignored him again, Peter turned back to Jessie. "Now what?"

"He's zoned. You'll have to pick him up and take him out."

"Will he cry?" he asked softly, probably so Jake wouldn't hear.

"Count on it."

"He's used to you. Maybe you should do it."

She gave him a lifted eyebrow. "He'll cry for me, too. Just make it clean and fast."

Peter put the towel down. Broad shoulders hunched, he leaned over the tub, poised to snatch the boy and lift him out of the water in his large, masculine hands. Strong and gentle, nails clean and neatly cut.

Neil's hands had been strong and gentle, too. Sometimes, they'd been cracked and stained from hard farm work even though he used the special soaps she'd given him. Her heart twisted at the memory of her ex-fiancé. "Okay. Go ahead," she encouraged.

Peter made his move.

With a shriek, Jake's chubby legs flailed, his slippery body squirming and twisting to get free.

"Whoa, there," Peter grunted, no doubt surprised by

the power one little boy could unleash. He tried to set Jake on his feet on the towel, but churning legs and a squirming body made that impossible. So Peter hugged Jake close instead. "It's okay, Jake. We're going to get you dry and dressed so you can have that snack."

At least his instincts were good. But it was hard to tell whether Jake heard him. He wailed loud enough to alert Jessie's parents on the patio. She wouldn't be surprised if Mom popped in to find out what was going on. "Calm down, sweetie," she cooed as she tucked the towel around Jake.

"He's never going to forgive me for doing that," Peter said dismally.

Jessie could almost feel sorry for the man...if she wasn't worried what he would decide to do when he fell in love with Jake. If he hadn't already.

Finally, Jake's crying subsided. "Wan Os," he said on a hiccough.

Peter looked over Jake's head at her as if asking her to interpret.

"He wants Cheerios for his snack." She nodded to let him know Os were an option.

"Sure, Jake. Os sound good," Peter said.

"Wan Os, wan Os." Jake sniffed, twisting to get out of Peter's arms.

"Slow down," Jessie warned. "You can have Os just as soon as Peter gets you into your diaper and pajamas."

Peter's eyebrows shot up. "You sure I'm up to that?"

"Aren't you?"

He squinted. "How hard can it be?"

Looked like he wasn't ready to cry uncle anytime soon. She laid a diaper and pj's on the changing table in the corner of the small room and stepped out of the way.

Peter climbed to his feet, abandoned the towel and laid Jake on the changing table without a hitch. He picked up the diaper, turning it in his hands as he studied it.

Not one to stay still for long, Jake began rolling onto his side.

Jessie lunged toward him.

"Whoa, there, fella." Peter grabbed Jake to stop him from falling.

Jessie gave a sigh of relief.

"You need to lie down, so I can get this diaper on you," Peter explained as if he expected the eighteen month old's complete cooperation.

"Wan Os." Jake swayed his head and upper torso back and forth to make his point.

"After we get you dressed," Peter said.

Jake wailed, struggling to free himself.

Jessie grabbed the towels on the floor and began wiping up the water near the tub. If Peter wanted her help, he could ask for it. But she kept a keen eye on his progress.

He held a squirming Jake with one hand while he spread the diaper on the changing table with the other. Then he plunked Jake on the diaper and somehow got it between the little boy's legs, but he couldn't seem to figure out how to fasten it. At least, not before Jake kicked free of the diaper and sent it flying.

Things couldn't be working out better. Suppressing a grin, Jessie flipped the drain and scooped toys into the net bag attached to the wall. "Are you going to get that diaper on him or not?"

Peter raked his free hand through his hair. "A demonstration might expedite things."

"Are you asking for my help?"

"Please?" He gave her a pathetic look. Well, as pathetic as a strong, handsome, intelligent man can look, anyway.

With an exaggerated sigh, she ambled over to contain Jake while Peter retrieved the diaper from the floor and laid it on the changing table.

Jessie gave Jake a toy car to keep him occupied, lifted him onto the diaper and secured it.

"You sure make it look easy," Peter commented.

"Experience. Can you handle putting him in his pajamas?"

Peter picked up the train-printed pj's and looked them over. "Snaps go back or front?"

"Front." She took the garment and matched top to bottom to show him.

"Got it."

She wiped down the tub-surround, glancing back to see how things were going.

Shoulders flexing, Peter worked to get the small, struggling boy into his pajamas, then concentrated on matching snaps. "We're almost finished, Jake," he promised several times.

Jessie perched on the side of the tub to wait. He must be realizing he wasn't cut out for parenting by now. One would think, anyway.

Finally, he lifted Jake in the air as he checked his work. "Mission accomplished," he announced. He did look like he'd been on a mission—a very wet one. His dark hair was soaked and as mussed as short hair can get, and his soaked shirt clung to his chest.

Jessie noticed one lone, unmatched snap on Jake's

pajamas and considered not mentioning it. But only for a second. "You missed a snap."

"Are you sure?" He gave her an exasperated look as he folded Jake in his arms.

"Of course I'm sure." She reached for Jake before his dry pajamas were as sodden as Peter was.

Jake hurled himself into her arms. "Wan Os, Mama."

"Okay." She concentrated on righting the snap and tried not to feel sorry for Peter in his wet shirt, but she did anyway. "If you want me to throw your shirt in the washer, you can wear one of Dad's."

He looked down at his soggy shirt. "That would be great. But I doubt your father wants me wearing his clothes."

"He won't mind." She opened the bathroom closet her mom had converted from linen storage to hold her dad's clothes. "Take your pick."

Giving her a wary eye, he chose a worn denim one she hadn't seen Dad wear for years. "This looks comfortable. It isn't his favorite, is it?"

Jessie shook her head.

Peter hung the hanger on the shower curtain rod and unbuttoned his shirt. He glanced at Jessie.

She realized she was watching as if a good-looking man taking off his shirt in her bathroom was an everyday occurrence. And not just any man…but the man who'd made a baby with her sister? "I'll just…uh…" She motioned toward the door.

He raised an eyebrow.

Flustered, she set Jake on his feet on the floor and darted out of the room after him. Well, wasn't that just lovely? Now Peter would probably think she was attracted to him.

Well, what woman wouldn't be? After all, he was a very attractive man, wasn't he?

By the time she got to the kitchen, Jake was pushing a chair to the cupboard. "I'll get your Os for you." She took the box from the cupboard and grabbed a small bowl from another shelf.

Peter strode into the room, powerful and in charge but looking a tad more relaxed in Dad's old shirt. His own wet shirt in his hand, he stopped by the table and studied the wall of family pictures. "Looks like you were a busy girl in school. Plays, proms, cheerleader."

She looked up from pouring cereal. "You know which pictures are me and which are Clarissa?"

"Sure." He turned to her. "You're very different from your sister, you know."

"She's the brainy one. No surprise there."

"You're brainy enough." Peter laid his shirt on the table to help Jake scramble into his high chair. He attempted to attach the tray without success. "You don't seem as driven as Clarissa. You're gentle. And there's more compassion in your eyes."

Strangely touched by his comment, she leaned in, clicked the tray in place and set the dish of cereal on it.

"People love you," he said.

She didn't know how to respond. "Why do you think that? You don't even know me."

"I've watched you with people. They love you."

"A problem when you can't live up to it."

He chuckled. "You have nothing to worry about, then."

She frowned. Did he take her comment as her attempt at humor? Or arrogance? If only. But how refreshing. He didn't know or care about her past or how far she'd fallen from the self-sufficient, independent woman she'd been before the accident. And he had no clue how much she had to depend on her parents and relatives to help her make her life run.

But his comments gave her the courage to ask a few personal questions of her own. "You said you and Clarissa were never a couple. That you don't have time for relationships. But obviously, you cared about each other…"

"Your sister and I had an excellent working relationship. We respected each other's integrity a great deal. We understood each other's drive and dedication to our work."

Jake held an O out to Peter.

"For me?" Peter bent and opened his mouth to let Jake drop the cereal inside.

Jake watched with rapt attention. "Mmm?"

"Mmm," Peter repeated.

A mixture of emotions churning inside her, Jessie waited for Peter to continue his explanation of his and Clarissa's relationship. But he didn't. Instead, she watched him and Jake take turns sharing Jake's snack. Finally, she decided to push the issue. Somehow, she needed to know. "Did you love her?"

Peter looked at Jessie, his smile disappearing. "It wasn't like that, Jessie."

She frowned. Clarissa had never given her the idea that she'd loved Jake's father, either. "How was it, then, Peter?"

He blew out a breath, clearly uncomfortable with the subject. "I guess you deserve some explanation. Clarissa and I were working together on an important experiment. When it failed, we were devastated. We took comfort in each other that night. That's it. It was a mistake.

It only happened once. Neither of us pursued anything further. Two months later, she transferred to the New York lab to further her career.

"I wished her well. I never suspected for a moment she was leaving to hide her pregnancy from me. I heard she took family leave a few months later to help her sister—you—recover from a car accident."

"Yes." She couldn't explain why she was relieved to hear their relationship had been mostly professional.

Jake held his arms up to Peter. "Hole me, 'kay?"

"I sure will." Peter beamed at Jake as if the heavens had opened up and showered him with manna. He fiddled to unsnap the tray, tugging it impatiently.

Jessie let him figure out the high chair on his own this time.

The tray unsnapped and came off in Peter's hands. Surprised, he looked it over.

Jake lunged out of his chair.

Jessie lurched to catch him, but she was too far away to reach him in time.

He hit the linoleum floor with a thud.

"Jake." Peter fell to his knees beside Jake.

"Mama," Jake wailed as soon as he caught his breath. "Need ice. Need ice."

Heart pounding, Jessie dropped beside him, scanning his head for bruises. "Will you get the ice pack from the freezer, Peter?"

"Right away." Pale and miserable, he climbed to his feet, strode to the fridge and yanked open the door.

She'd never get used to Jake getting hurt, even if she had learned to stay calm so she could help him. Noticing a spot on his forehead turning pink, she gathered him close. "The ice pack is in the door rack. Grab the dish towel on the oven door to wrap it in."

He was back in a flash and handed her the towel-wrapped ice with shaking hands.

She held it to Jake's head.

Jake reached to help her hold the pack. "Pedo hurt Jake," he accused.

Peter shut his eyes. "I'm so sorry."

"Peter didn't hurt you, honey," Jessie explained. "He didn't know you were going to jump."

Peter shook his head as if he couldn't believe his incompetence. "I shouldn't have taken my eyes off him."

Jessie's heart ached for Peter. "I should have warned you he likes to jump."

What had she been thinking? She'd been selfish and smug trying to show Peter he couldn't be a parent. He *was* a parent. A parent who wanted to know his son and his son to know him. Didn't every child deserve to know his daddy?

She'd die before she'd give Jake up. But that didn't mean she had to be selfish. If she held on too tight, she might lose Jake completely.

"He could have gotten seriously hurt," Peter said miserably.

She saw defeat in his eyes, defeat she'd wanted.

She felt terrible. Peter didn't deserve this. She'd been wrong.

Instead of being critical and acting superior, shouldn't she be helping Peter learn Jake's habits? Because no matter what, she had to do everything in her power to keep her little boy safe. "How many skills do you think I had when I brought him home from the hospital? But I learned."

"I'm sure Jake didn't get hurt while you were learning."

"He won't get hurt, Peter. Not if I teach you. You did say you're a quick study."

# Chapter Five

Trying to shut out the memory of Jake's fall, Peter sat at the rickety desk in a musty motel room he'd finally found on the outskirts of town. Seemed graduates' relatives had booked everything in the town's one decent motel and the B and B. He'd made a few calls and found another chemist to cover the tasks he'd planned to take care of this weekend. Now he stared at the graph he'd pulled up on his laptop while he explained the Jake situation to Scott on his cell.

"I'm shocked," Scott said. "I had no idea you were leading a secret life."

"Right." He knew Scott's remark was a stab at humor. "Like I have time for a secret life."

"Doesn't change the fact that you're a daddy. And knowing you, you're not taking it lightly."

He leaned his arm on the desk and propped his head in his hand. "I don't want my son growing up without a father like I did."

"Maybe you'll have to take my advice to hire more people at the lab, if you're actually contemplating a life outside of it."

And compromise his research? He wouldn't be even

close to the testing phase of the new drug without the countless hours he spent in the lab. "I need to be on top of things. You know that."

"So hire good people to help you stay on top of things."

"Good people leave just when you have them trained the way you want them."

"Like Clarissa did?"

"Obviously. I think she transferred to the New York lab because she wanted to hide her pregnancy from me. But other promising people have left for various reasons, too."

"You need to give them more responsibility. Stop trying to save the world all by yourself, man. It can't be done. Besides, good people need to feel they have a stake in the outcome."

"We've had this discussion before, Scott."

"To no avail. But you'll have to make some changes if you want to spend time with your son."

Peter closed his eyes against a flash of Jake falling. "I let him fall today. He moved so quickly, I didn't have time to react."

"Is he all right?"

"Yes, but I'm sure the bump on the little guy's head will impress his grandparents, especially when they learn I'm responsible for it. I should have anticipated his action. I'd seen him make a game of throwing himself with Jessie. Of course, she caught him. I should have."

"Don't be too hard on yourself, Peter. It's not like you've ever been around kids."

"But it could have been serious. The amazing thing is that Jessie didn't pounce on me. She doesn't want me here. She's made that abundantly clear. Yet, when Jake accused me of hurting him, Jessie defended me. She must have known if she didn't come to my aid, the kid would never trust me again. Maybe he still won't. But instead of blaming me, she promised to teach me how to take care of him."

"Maybe she's trying to protect the child."

"That makes sense. She really loves him. She lights up like a Christmas tree with him."

"She sounds like a wonderful, compassionate woman, Peter."

"Yeah. She looks like Clarissa, but the resemblance ends there. Jessie's soft, vulnerable. But with a core of steel, I'm finding out." He remembered his discomfort when she offered to pray. What would Scott think of it? "She said she'd pray for you and me."

"Did you thank her?"

Peter sighed. "I didn't know what to say. Nobody's offered to pray for me before."

"Karen and I always pray for you."

"What?" Peter shook his head. "You never told me that."

"I wasn't sure you'd be comfortable with the idea."

He was right about that. But at least, thanks to Scott, Peter now knew how to respond. "Thank you."

"You're very welcome."

Too bad he couldn't say he prayed for them...or that he knew how to pray at all, for that matter. "What should I do?"

"I've never been a father. What makes you think I can advise you on this?"

"You've been as close to a father as I've ever had. Nobody knows me better."

"I know you won't be able to live with yourself if you don't do everything possible for that little boy. You'll have to decide how much you need to be involved with him. What kind of dad do you want to be?"

Peter recognized the exhaustion in Scott's voice. He had to let him get off the phone soon, but he'd never needed his wisdom more. "I want him to know he can count on me, no matter what."

"That will take some serious relationship building."

"Not my strong suit, I know. Not to mention the time." Time he didn't have.

"Are you considering bringing him to live with you?" Scott asked.

"I don't know." Straightening, Peter rolled his shoulders to get out the kinks. "That could take a court battle."

"Not a happy prospect."

"The worst."

"Maybe you can work out something part-time with Jessie. Do you think she'd be willing to move to Madison so you can see more of him?"

Peter thought about it for a second. "I don't know. Her family's here. And she has her own business, a diner."

"Maybe you can help her establish a business in Madison or in one of the towns nearby."

That would make it possible for him to keep long hours in the lab and be part of Jake's life. And it wouldn't force him to tear his son from the only mother he'd ever known. But would Jessie consider moving? "I'll give it some thought."

"Figure out what you're willing to do for a relationship with your son. Once you know the answer to that question, you'll figure out the rest."

"I can see sleepless nights ahead. Thanks for listening. Now get some rest. I'll be home tomorrow."

"You know we wish you the best." Scott's phone clicked off.

Peter turned off his cell and stared at the graph on his laptop. He gave a fleeting thought to the list of tasks at the lab he'd had to delegate to allow him to stay another day. Too many things for his own peace of mind.

But Scott was right. To allow time for Jake, Peter would have to cut back on his hours. That would mean assigning some of his work to technicians and hiring another assistant to take up the slack. Was it possible to make so many changes without compromising the stringent quality he demanded in the lab? Especially now that they were beginning the testing phase on humans? He sure couldn't compromise that.

His mind snagged on the mathematical equation he'd been working out on his laptop. The roadblock shifting and giving way, he began keying in the solution.

If only he could solve his sudden father status as easily.

"What?" With a glance in each direction, Maggie power walked across the street beside Jessie. "Whatever made you decide to help him?"

Dragging in a breath of earthy scent left behind by the rain, Jessie hurried to keep pace. "He looked so defeated, I…"

"He manipulated you."

Is that what happened? Remembering the look on Peter's face after Jake fell, Jessie shook her head. "No, he didn't."

"Well, he took advantage of the situation to get you to do what he wants. Sounds like a controlling man to me." Maggie dodged a puddle in the middle of the sidewalk.

Jessie veered to avoid her. "What kind of mother would I be if I didn't make sure he knows how to keep Jake safe?"

"How much are you planning to let him be around Jake?"

"I don't know. Will advised me to compromise. He said if it goes to court, Peter could possibly win full custody if he wanted."

"How can you be certain he's Jake's father without a paternity test?"

"He already took swabs for a DNA test. But anyone can see he's Jake's father."

"Well, even so, waiting for results of the DNA test could buy you time until you figure out a strategy to deal with him."

"There's been no time to figure out a strategy," Jessie blurted. "It's like Jake and I are suddenly in the middle of a tornado and all I can think about is how to keep him safe."

"I don't mean to criticize, Jess. I just want to help."

"I know." Jessie waved at neighbors sitting on their front porch, the ache in her hip warning her to drop back a little.

Maggie slowed her pace. "You okay?"

"I'm fine." She wanted to tell the entire town she was fine and be done with it. After the accident, being grateful for everyone's concern had worked for a long time, but constant reminders that she was no longer the person she used to be only set her apart to pity.

Pity didn't help. Not pity from others, nor self-pity. She needed her energy to try to keep her life together.

Which she'd been doing a reasonable job of until Peter Sheridan showed up with a claim on Jake.

She couldn't help feeling God had pulled the rug out from under her...again.

Mixers whirring, Jessie hurried to one of the stoves, pulled two strawberry-rhubarb pies from the oven and set them on the cooling rack. Tossing her oven mitts on the counter, she barely noticed the mouth-watering aromas mingling with the other pies and cakes she'd managed to bake despite being all thumbs this morning. She gave the clock above the sink an evil eye. How had she forgotten she had extra baking to do when she'd pushed her snooze button the third time?

Of course, if she'd been able to sleep, she wouldn't have needed more z's. But she doubted sleepless nights or the anxiety that spurred them were going away any time soon. At least not while Peter Sheridan was in town.

She flipped off the mixers, grasped a bowl and rubber spatula and poured airy yellow batter for Mom's Sunshine Cake into the ungreased tube pan. Ever since she'd decided to teach Peter about Jake last night, she couldn't shake the feeling she was making it easier for him to steal her son from her. Her conversation with Maggie during their nightly walk hadn't helped. But what else could she do? She had to protect Jake.

"Smells good in here." Jessie's mom walked through the kitchen.

"Hi, Mom." Blowing the tendril of hair out of her eyes that had somehow escaped her kerchief, Jessie poured batter for Aunt Lou's walnut cake into the prepared pan.

"You look so stressed, dear."

"Not what I need to hear, Mom." Grasping both cake pans, Jessie strode to the oven, popped them in and set the timer. "I'm muddling through with only a few minor mishaps."

"I see." She spotted Jessie's earlier attempt at Sunshine Cake on the counter. "New recipe for lemon pancakes?"

"Ha," she said half-heartedly. It was pretty obvious she'd been too distracted to beat something long enough, probably the egg whites. She checked the clock. Her mom was running late, too.

"You know stress isn't good for you, Jess."

Jessie blew out a breath of impatience. "I'm fine."

Mom washed and dried her hands at the sink. "Sometimes it's okay not to be fine."

"*Now* is not that time."

"All right." Her mom threw up her hands as if giving up.

Jessie didn't believe it for a second. "Lots of people stayed in town after graduation yesterday. We'll have even longer lines waiting at the door than we usually do on Sunday mornings. I haven't had time to start coffee or set up out front yet."

"I'm on it." She grasped the cash drawer Jessie had gotten ready earlier. "Your dad promised to bring Jake in plenty of time to allow me to get him settled for his nap before church. By the way, the bump on Jake's head was barely visible this morning."

Jessie dragged in a breath, remembering Jake's fall. Noticing the fatigue on her mother's face, Jessie's heart contracted. Her mom was stressed, too. Of course, what Peter did affected her parents, too.

*Please don't take Jake from us, God. I don't know what any of us would do without him.* She pressed her fingers to her forehead to try to stop the flood of emotions. Her head felt like it might explode. "Do you think we could lose Jake, Mom?"

"Oh, honey…" Her mother set down the cash drawer and gave Jessie a hug, then drew back and met her eyes. "After you told us about Peter's life last night, I can't imagine he thinks he can take care of Jake."

With her heart aching, Jessie shook her head. "If only I'd left it alone after Jake's fall…but I couldn't. He's Jake's daddy, and whether we like it or not, there's nothing we can do to change that." Jessie bit her lip. "It would be so much easier if he didn't seem like a good man who wants to do the right thing."

"You don't mean that, Jess. You wouldn't want a bad father for Jake."

"No. But it *would* make it a lot easier to dislike Peter. As it is, I keep thinking, what little boy doesn't need his daddy? Especially one who's so interested in him?" She felt sick to her stomach. "But I'll never forgive myself if I've set things in motion to give Peter the confidence he needs to take Jake away."

Mom patted her arm. "We need to put the situation in God's hands, dear."

"How can you be so confident…after what happened to Clarissa?"

Mom gave her a sad smile. "I pray the gospel prayer, 'Lord, I believe. Help thou mine unbelief.'"

Faith seemed so simple when Mom talked about it. Jessie blew out a breath. Why did she find it so difficult?

When nobody answered the door at Jessie's home, Peter drove to the diner. He was anxious to see Jake. He sure hoped the little guy had forgiven him for letting him fall last night. Peter was jazzed about taking him to play at the children's park he'd seen near one of the schools. With Jessie's supervision, of course. He didn't trust himself to go solo, and he doubted she would, either.

But who would have guessed he'd have to wait in a long line of chattering people to get into Jessie's Main Street Diner to see his son? Finally edging inside the noisy place, enticing smells confirmed Jessie's food was a lot better than the late, so-called dinner he'd eaten near the motel last night. Probably the reason she had so many customers standing in line.

The young woman he'd seen behind the counter yesterday—Lisa—gave him a nod of acknowledgment from her post at the cash register.

He broke from the line. "Is Jake in the back room?"

Lisa frowned. "You'll have to talk to Jessie about Jake."

Peering over people's heads, he spotted Jessie alone behind the counter and headed for her.

A big guy threw out his arm to stop him. "You'll have to wait in line like everybody else, buddy."

Peter glanced around as customers closed ranks, preventing him from reaching the counter. "I'm not here to eat," he tried to explain to the scowling crowd.

"Then you're in the wrong place," the big man supplied helpfully.

Peter turned to Lisa, who glanced away. Didn't look as if he'd get much help there, which made him wish he hadn't been so pushy with her yesterday when he'd demanded to see Jake. He glanced at the bright, butterfly-patterned curtain that, no doubt, hid his son from him. He'd need a tank to cut through the wall-to-wall customers between him and the curtain.

It didn't look like he had a lot of choices. He could either start a riot or wait his turn and talk to Jessie at the counter. He settled in for the duration. How long could it take?

Unfortunately, twenty minutes later, the bell over the door still tinkled nonstop, chatter bounced off the old tin ceiling tiles like Ping-Pong balls and Peter still waited in line. The only change was that the delicious smells rising from the grill made his stomach growl with hunger. Maybe he'd have breakfast after all.

Behind the counter, Jessie looked pretty and cheerful in a denim skirt and pink T-shirt with a matching kerchief tying back her hair. She moved as fluidly as a well-trained dancer going through her paces, her limp barely noticeable. She interacted with many of her customers as if they were longtime friends. They probably were.

The tall, unfriendly guy Peter met coming out of Jessie's back room yesterday eyed him from his seat at the counter. Whatever the guy's relationship with her was, the way he looked at her told Peter he wanted it to be more. But Jessie's demeanor said "just friends." Funny how much that insight pleased Peter.

Finally, a woman vacated her red vinyl stool.

Being next in line, Peter claimed it, catching Jessie's eye as he sat down.

A frown chasing away her smile, she cleared away the dishes in front of him.

"Good morning," he said, noting the wariness in her blue eyes. She wasn't wearing even the touch of makeup she'd worn yesterday. He had the fleeting urge to reach out and touch her smooth, inviting skin. What would she do if he did?

"Coffee?"

"Black, thanks."

She grasped the coffee pot and filled his cup, her hand shaking enough to slosh a little on the counter.

He hated that he made her nervous. "Thank you. Rough morning?"

"You could say that." Without meeting his eyes, she whipped a menu from its holder, handed it to him, then moved on to the next customer to fill his cup.

Not exactly friendly. He hoped that didn't mean she'd changed her mind about teaching him how to handle Jake. Sipping great coffee, Peter studied the menu, his gaze wandering to Jessie turning eggs and sausage on the grill, scooping orders onto plates and delivering them to customers. Compassion, efficiency and a great cook wrapped in a very pretty package. He couldn't help wondering why she was still single.

Finally, she stopped in front of him. "Have you decided what you'd like?"

"Is Jake in the back?"

"Yes. He's napping." Her eyes looked pinched as if she could use a nap, too.

"Can I have some more coffee down here, Jess?" a deep voice boomed.

Jessie jumped as if she'd been caught playing hooky, grabbed the coffee pot and hurried to take care of the demanding customer.

Sipping his coffee, Peter watched her tend the grill, serve customers, hand out checks and clear away dishes from the counter without missing a beat. She headed his way with the coffeepot in hand.

She filled his cup. "Do you know what you'd like?"

"I'll have number nine on the menu. How long will Jake sleep?"

"Judging by how tired he was, at least a couple hours." She moved along the counter filling customers' cups.

Peter sighed. At this rate, it would take him all morning to make plans with Jessie to play with Jake.

"You picked the wrong time to try to talk to her." The hefty man with thinning hair on Peter's right took a final bite of toast.

Peter gave the man a look to discourage his interest.

"She's got her routine down to an art form," the man said. "And she doesn't like to be interrupted."

The look hadn't worked. Peter felt a little on the cranky side for lack of sleep, and he was only too aware he was wasting valuable time away from his research.

"I'm Jessie's uncle Harold."

Great. He'd been rude to her uncle. Peter turned to the man wearing a white shirt and tie and stuck out his hand. "Peter Sheridan."

Harold wiped his fingers on his napkin before he shook Peter's hand. "I know who you are. So does most of Noah's Crossing. Your name was on everybody's lips at church fellowship this morning."

What were they doing? Praying for him, too? That couldn't be good, could it?

"How long are you staying?" Jessie's uncle asked.

"I need to head home tonight."

Harold pushed his empty plate away and held Peter's gaze. "Jessie's been through some real tough times. We almost lost her in a bad car accident a couple years ago. Then her sister died. Little Jake means the world to her and her folks. I hope you're not planning to bring more heartache to that family."

Peter sighed. He should have guessed Jessie's accident had been life-threatening. It probably explained her limp, too. And gave added credence to Clarissa's decision to take personal leave and come home for her baby's birth. What if she hadn't? If she'd stayed in New York, maybe she would never have told her family about Jake, either. "I want to be a father to my son, that's all."

"Commendable. How you planning to do that from Madison?"

Peter narrowed his eyes. Jessie's uncle or not, he wanted to ask the man what business any of this was of his.

Jessie set a plate of scrambled eggs, bacon and toast in front of Peter that smelled as good as it looked. "Uncle Harold, can you handle the cash register until Aunt Lou gets here, please?"

Peter glanced to the empty spot where Lisa had stood.

"Where's Lisa?" Jessie's uncle asked.

"She's not feeling well."

Harold gave a nod. "Morning sickness."

Busy clearing Harold's used dishes, Jessie snapped her head around. "Lisa's pregnant?"

"That's what Lou says."

Jessie frowned as if the news was anything but joyful. "But little Denise is only nine months old."

"Surprises happen, Jess."

Shaking her head, she hustled away with the dishes.

Peter was surprised by Jessie's reaction to the news of a baby on the way. The way she was with Jake, she had to love babies.

Jessie wiped the counter in front of her uncle.

"I'll get right on that register. And Lou should be finishing up leading her Bible study about now," Harold said. "She'll be here soon so you can leave like you planned, Jess."

"Thank you," she said.

It sounded like Jessie had already made time for him and Jake to be together. Peter took a bite of tasty bacon.

Harold stood and gave Peter's shoulder a couple thumps. "Glad to meet you, Peter."

"Same here," Peter said absently. He was anxious to talk to Jessie about taking Jake to the park.

Harold walked away as a tall man in work overalls took the stool beside Peter.

Jessie set a glass of orange juice on the counter for Peter and topped off his coffee. "Anything else I can get you?"

Peter didn't waste any time. "I was thinking we could take Jake to the playground this morning."

"We can take him for a little while if you want, but I won't be free until after one."

"But your uncle just said you could leave soon."

"Aunt Lou and Mom will take over here so I can go to the late church service."

"Do you take Jake with you?"

"Sometimes. When he takes a shorter nap than today. But we can meet you at the park on Maple about one-thirty."

"One-thirty? Church lasts that long?"

"After church, I need to finish things up here. I close the diner at noon on Sundays."

Peter shut his eyes, trying to rein in his frustration. "I was hoping I could spend time with Jake this morning, then get on the road back to the lab."

"I'm sorry, Peter. One-thirty is the best I can do." With that, she hurried away again.

Peter stared at his breakfast, his appetite gone. Sure, Jessie had promised to teach him about Jake, but she controlled the entire situation. And it was pretty obvious she had no idea the limited time he had to spend with his son.

If he was going to be a real part of Jake's life, he couldn't just wait around for her to call all the shots. He needed to take control and find a way to make things happen.

# Chapter Six

Sun warm on her head, Jessie peered through the lens, waiting for the perfect picture. Bringing her camera to the park had been an afterthought. A thought that seemed to lift Peter out of the glum mood he'd left the diner with this morning. He'd seemed surprised she planned to snap a few pictures of him with Jake.

Truth was, sitting in church she'd had a conscience attack of sorts. God had helped her see that Peter hadn't deliberately set out to ruin her life. He was, after all, only trying to deal with a difficult situation, wasn't he? How many men would handle it as well as he was? Especially one with his heavy responsibilities?

So maybe she could cut him a break. Maybe try being a little nicer.

She snapped a picture of him pushing Jake in the child's swing. A memory of Neil pushing his nephew in a swing flitted into Jessie's mind. Her heart ached for the happy days they'd shared...for the life they'd planned...for the family they'd never have.

*Don't go there, Jessie.*

She clicked the lens. "Good one." The giant man;

the tiny boy. The father and his miniature, lookalike son. Any mother would be hard pressed to find a more touching subject.

Lowering the camera, she watched them interact. They were already bonding, no question about that. A twinge of loss nudged her. Jake had belonged only to her and her family before Peter showed up. Would she have to give him up? Would she learn to share him?

What must it be like to completely share a child? To conceive a baby with the man you loved, to share the baby's growth in your womb, to experience the birth together? Like her younger cousin Lisa would be doing. Again. *I want to be happy for her, God. I do. But she already has her adorable little Denise. And now she gets to experience the whole miracle all over again.* Throat closing, she concentrated on snapping another picture.

Peter twisted the swing and let Jake spin.

Jake squealed with laughter.

Jessie cringed. A little too rough for her taste, even if her dad did remind her Jake was a sturdy boy every time they roughhoused. She raised the camera and snapped a picture.

Peter lifted the swing above his head, his long, lean body stretching to the sky, his muscular legs planted firmly on the ground.

Jessie took a quick breath, her fingers taking a couple extra seconds to find the button on the camera.

"Want an underduck, Jake?" Peter asked.

"Undaduck!" Jake shouted.

All muscles and action, Peter ran under the swing and let it go.

Jake screeched with laughter, the swing flying far too high.

Jessie clicked the lens. "That's too high for him, Peter."

"He loves going high."

"But if his head jerks back, he could injure his neck."

Peter frowned.

"Pedo! More undaduck!" Jake swung more slowly now.

Peter glanced at Jessie.

She shook her head. "He doesn't know what's safe and what isn't. That's our job." *Our* job? She sounded as if they were a real family. A real family just having everyday fun together. What must that be like?

"Pedo! Undaduck!"

Peter stepped close to Jake and gave him a modified underduck. "Better?"

Jessie nodded, relieved he'd deferred to her with Jake's safety.

"Pedo! *Big* undaduck!"

Peter chuckled. "Can't do, fella. *You* have to get bigger for that."

Jake pulled his pout.

Time for distraction. "You want to go on the slide?" Jessie asked.

"Slide." Jake drew his legs up and tried to stand in the swing.

Jessie tensed.

Thankfully, Peter grabbed him before he could fall. "You're a little daredevil."

"Pedo divil?" Jake patted Peter's face.

Peter laughed.

Jessie snapped a picture. "Don't forget, words you teach him will come back to bite you."

"No doubt." Peter lifted Jake over his head to straddle his shoulders.

Fully appreciating the view in her lens, she snapped a great picture.

"Is it my imagination or are little kids a breath away from disaster at any given moment?" Peter asked.

Jessie narrowed her eyes. "Do you think I worry too much about him?"

"In a good way."

She met his smiling eyes, her stomach doing a little flip. He looked so much happier than he had yesterday. "Dad says I'll make a hothouse flower out of him."

Jake began bouncing on Peter's shoulders.

Peter grasped his legs more firmly. "I doubt there's much danger of Jake becoming a hothouse flower."

She laughed, glad to hear another male's opinion on Jake. "I'll tell my father you said that the next time he teases me."

Peter ran his gaze over her face. "You have a nice laugh."

"Thank you." She inwardly cringed at the breathiness in her voice. Might as well flash a neon sign announcing "Aware and Interested Female Here." Which wasn't true. She'd given up that dream when Neil broke off their engagement.

Her dream of a husband and family wasn't all the accident stole from her. After her broken engagement and Clarissa's death, everybody looked at her in a whole new way than they had when she was the cheerleader dating the town's prize athlete, the prom- and homecoming queen, the girl voted most likely to succeed in whatever she did. Now, they saw her as a victim who needed help. She hated it.

Somehow, Peter made her feel like that whole person again. It was nice to be around someone besides Jake who didn't feel sorry for her. She sighed. But who knew what the man was planning behind those rich brown eyes?

Reaching for a new train of thought, she pointed to the slide. "I'll take your picture with Jake on the ladder. But the slide's too high for him to go down alone."

"I can't remember the last time I was on one of those things." Peter headed for the ladder, posed at the top with Jake, then stretched his long legs in front of him and zipped down the slide with Jake in his lap. Peter's deep laugh resonated along with Jake's squeals.

Jessie couldn't help smiling.

"Would you like me to take a picture of you with your lovely little family?" a small, white-haired woman sitting on a nearby park bench offered.

Jessie should correct the woman's mistake, but instead, she found herself handing her the camera. "That's very kind."

Peter carried Jake across the grass.

"Peter, this kind lady has offered to take a picture of us."

"Okay." Giving Jessie a lopsided grin, he moved closer to her and focused on the camera.

Jessie smiled, hanging on to the illusion of a real family as if a picture could make it true. She heard the camera click. "Thank you so much."

"You're very welcome." The smiling woman returned the camera and strolled away.

"Run." Jake squirmed to get down.

"He can't get hurt running on the soft grass, can he?" Peter asked.

"Not unless he trips and falls."

He raised a dark eyebrow. "Are you kidding?"

"Mostly. He's very sure-footed. He's been running on his toes ever since he took his first steps at nine months."

Peter set him down.

Jake took off, his chubby legs churning across the grass.

Jessie kept her eye on him. "I used to hold my breath every time he hurled himself across the floor. His legs didn't always keep up with his body."

"I'm sorry I missed that."

Her heart clutched. He'd missed so many important things in his son's life. "I'm sorry, too, Peter."

He met her eyes. "I appreciate that."

"Every father deserves to see his child's firsts. I have tons of pictures of him. I'll show them to you and make copies of whatever you want."

"I'd like that very much." His gaze roamed her face as if he couldn't quite size her up. "Mind if I use your camera?"

"Be my guest." She handed the camera to him, his fingers brushing hers.

Warmth zinged through her.

He met her eyes.

Had he felt it, too? She managed to look away.

He took a shot of Jake running. When Jake noticed Peter clicking the camera, he headed straight for it.

"What a little ham." Laughing, Jessie dropped to her knees to catch him, then swooped him into the air and gave his tummy a buzz.

Jake giggled out of control.

She lowered him to nuzzle noses and heard the camera click.

Jake struggled to break away from her. "Jake run!"

She set him on the ground and watched him run away.

Camera hanging around his neck, Peter walked over to her and hung his hands on his narrow hips, his white shirt pulling across his chest. "He's a great kid."

"Yes, he is." They sounded like any parents talking about their child. Having someone to share Jake's life with her could be a good thing, couldn't it? And Peter seemed very different from the anxious man at the lectern yesterday. Or for that matter, the one who'd left the diner in a funk this morning. "I think fatherhood agrees with you."

"Yeah? Can you see me with a whole houseful of little Jakes? Maybe a few pretty little girls thrown in for good measure?" He laughed.

Heart skidding to a standstill, she drew in a deep breath of reality. "You want a family?"

"In my dreams." He gave her a self-deprecating little smile. "In the real world, I have yet to figure out how I'm going to fit Jake into my life."

She knew all about dreams. But she could daydream they'd make a happy little family till the cows came home, and it wouldn't change a thing. Any man who loved children would want more than one.

He'd want a woman who could give them to him. And Jessie couldn't.

That evening, Peter followed Jessie and Jake down the narrow hall with more than a little trepidation. Sure, things had gone better than he'd expected this afternoon. And tucking Jake in for the night sounded simple enough, but who knew what pitfalls lay hidden in a small boy's rituals?

He didn't want to do anything that might hinder Jake's budding trust in him. Especially not when he had to head back to Madison tonight and didn't know when he'd be able to get away to see the little guy again.

Jessie bringing her camera to the park had surprised and pleased him. She'd even come out of her shell and appeared to accept him a little. He'd thought about asking her if she'd consider moving Jake to Madison, but the time hadn't seemed right. He needed to find out before he left, though. It was the only way he'd know how to proceed.

Walking into the small bedroom, he couldn't help smiling. Jessie had made sure Jake had everything a little boy could possibly need. A crib, a rocking chair, a book shelf loaded with books, a low train table and two big wooden train cars brimming with toys, undoubtedly Jessie's dad's work. A red stripe ran chair-rail height around the room with brightly painted, wood trains hanging on the medium-blue wall above.

Her silky hair veiling her face, Jessie bent and plucked a book from the shelf. "Peter will read your favorite story."

Peter waited, wondering if the boy would object.

Instead, Jake held out his arms to him.

Feeling like king of the mountain, Peter picked him up. But the small bruise on the little guy's forehead did a quick job of dashing his ego. Good thing for him that eighteen-month-olds apparently regained trust more easily than adults did.

Jessie handed Peter a little book and indicated he should sit in the rocking chair.

Peter sat down and carefully positioned Jake on his lap.

"Tomut." Jake pointed at the little blue engine on the cover.

"I see. The book is about your engine."

"Story." Jake opened the book, ready to get down to business.

Needing no further direction, Peter began to read.

Jake listened with rapt attention, identifying pictures in his own language.

Smart kid. And Peter could mostly figure out what he was saying by matching his words to pictures in the book.

"End." Jake slammed the book shut. "More story."

"No," Jessie said. "Now Peter will rock you and sing a song."

A song? Peter shot her a look. "I'm tone deaf."

"Jake isn't fussy."

"Easy for you to say." He frowned at her. "I don't know any songs."

"He loves it when I make one up."

She expected Peter to make up a song? She didn't understand. He wasn't just marginally musically challenged. He was tone deaf. Melody deaf. Completely unable to make up songs. Period.

Jake twisted around and held up his arms.

Peter lifted him against his chest.

Jake snuggled close and laid his head on Peter's shoulder. "Pedo sing, 'kay?"

Peter's heart contracted. No way could he turn Jake down. He scoured his brain for a song to sing to a little kid. He knew all the words to one. He glanced at Jessie. "Don't say I didn't warn you." Stroking Jake's back, he decided to go for it. "Happy birthday to you," he intoned in his rusty monotone.

Bless him, Jake began to hum along.

Jessie turned and busied herself arranging the bookshelf but not before Peter saw the grin on her face. At least she had the decency not to laugh out loud.

His voice was even worse than he remembered. But Jake's little hum in his ear kept him going to the finish. "Happy birthday, Thomas the Tank Engine, happy birthday to you."

Jake's head popped up from Peter's shoulder, a megawatt smile on his face. "Tomut?"

Peter smiled right back.

"You're a hit," Jessie said.

"You were right. He's not fussy about his music."

A hint of a smile lifted the corners of her mouth. "Time for bed now, Jake."

Jake shook his head. "Pedo sing."

"I don't know any more songs," Peter explained.

"Sing Tomut."

"Time for sleep," Jessie insisted. "Peter will put you in your bed, right Peter?"

"Sure will." Peter stood and set Jake in his crib.

"Sing, Pedo?" Jake squinted up at him.

"Sorry, big guy. Time to sleep now."

"Give him a hug and this." Jessie handed Peter a soft, blue blanket.

Peter followed her coaching.

Jake dropped the blanket in his bed without looking at it.

Jessie stepped close to the crib and gave Jake a hug. "Good night, sweetie. See you in the morning."

Jake reached his arms out to Peter. "Pedo, hole me, 'kay?"

Peter looked to Jessie.

She gave her head a little shake. "Tell him good night."

"Good night, Jake."

"Story, Pedo."

Peter would have thought the boy was too young to know about manipulation, let alone how to use it. Effectively, too.

"Let's go." Jessie walked out of the room.

Peter followed.

She pulled the door mostly closed. "I leave the door open a crack so I can hear him if he needs me."

So parenting really was 24/7. He walked down the hall beside Jessie. Now that Jake was in bed, he needed to concentrate on how to bring up the subject to Jessie of moving to Madison.

"Pedo," Jake called from his doorway. "More Tomut."

"Uh-oh. Now what?" Peter asked under his breath.

"Be firm. Put him in his crib, then leave the room."

Peter strode back, careful not to meet Jake's eyes as he picked up the little guy and plunked him in his crib.

"Pedo," Jake wailed from his crib.

Peter hated this. "You have to go to sleep now, Jake." Steeling himself, he turned and walked out of the room to join Jessie. "I think he's working up to real tears."

Jessie shook her head. "It didn't take."

"Pedo!" Jake yelled gleefully from the doorway.

"He had me fooled," Peter admitted. "And he's fast."

"He's testing to see what you'll do."

"Any suggestions?"

"Don't give in no matter what, or there will be problems with bedtime."

"Good point." Peter strode for the doorway, purpose in his step. He swooped Jake up, put him back in bed and walked out of the room. Several seconds later, so did Jake. Peter retraced his footsteps again. And again. And again.

Jessie just stood in the hall, patiently waiting for Peter to show Jake who was in charge.

Quite the challenge, but finally, Jake stayed put. The only sound coming from his room was his small voice. "Is he singing?"

"He sings to his toys." Jessie began walking down the hall. "He'll be asleep in no time. Good job of hanging tough."

"Thanks." Hanging tough with Jake was a lot more difficult than he'd imagined, but Jessie seemed to think he'd handled himself pretty well. That had to count for something. Peter ambled behind her into the tidy kitchen. "I'm getting the idea parenting takes lots of perseverance."

"Perseverance, consistency, time…"

"Aw, yes, time. Point taken." He glanced at the clock hanging above the sink. "Speaking of time, I need to get on the road." But he still hadn't asked her about moving Jake to Madison. He sure hoped she'd be more cooperative than Jake had been. "Will you walk me to my car?"

She shot him a questioning look.

"I'd like to talk more about Jake."

With a nod, she slid open the screen door and stepped onto the patio.

Peter followed her into the warm night, the frogs' serenade increasing in volume. He walked beside her toward the driveway, mentally preparing the best way to ask his question.

"'Happy Birthday' was the only song you could think of?" she chided.

"You can make fun, but you didn't have a choral teacher tell you not to sing when you were twelve."

"Did *you?*"

"Oh, yeah. To her credit, she tried to teach me to sing. But finally, she declared me tone deaf and told me to just mouth the words because I confused singers around me."

"What an awful thing for her to do."

"Actually, I was relieved. I needed the art credit, and singing wouldn't have helped me get it." Peter watched several fireflies blinking their way through the dusk.

"Well, Jake loves music. So tone deaf or not, I'll teach you some kid songs."

Stopping at his car, he caught the fresh, lemon scent of her hair. "Thank you for helping me with him, Jessie."

She bit her lip. "Teaching you about Jake is in his best interest, don't you agree?"

"Definitely." Of course, she was teaching him for Jake. But she was putting her own interests aside to do it. A delightful and unexpected surprise. He had the feeling she was full of unexpected surprises. Maybe agreeing to move Jake to Madison would be one of them. "I've been doing some thinking about finding time for Jake in my life. I need to know…is there any chance you'd consider moving with him to Madison?"

"What?" Her eyes drilled into him. "Why would I consider doing that?"

Seemed obvious to him. "So I can spend time with him and be a real father."

She frowned. "After the accident, I moved home to be close to my family. My business, my life is here now.

Why would I give all that up to move to a city I don't
know, with people I haven't met and for a job I don't
have?"

He didn't know how to answer that. "It's pretty obvious I can't do research in Noah's Crossing. I can't leave
Scott, either. But you don't need to give me an answer
right now. Will you think about it?"

"I don't need to think about it." She set her chin.

"I can afford to help you get your own business up
and running either in Madison or in a small town nearby
if that's what you want to do."

"Peter…in case you haven't noticed, I depend on my
family to help me keep everything running with Jake
and my business."

"You can hire help in Madison."

"Strangers?" She gave him a dismissive look. "Besides, what makes you think I'd accept financial help
from you?"

Rubbing the back of his neck, Peter tried to wrap his
mind around Jessie's unwillingness to compromise. "We
both want what's best for Jake, right?"

"Of course I want what's best for Jake. But moving
him away from everything and everybody he knows and
loves is not it."

"He's eighteen months old. I'm sure he'll adapt."

"Why can't you drive up on weekends to see him?"

Peter pinched the bridge of his nose in an attempt to
think clearly. "How can I be the father he needs if I'm
with him only a few hours on weekends?"

"I don't know, Peter. But moving to Madison is impossible." She shook her head. "Out of the question."
Turning on her heel, she strode across the yard to the
house.

He watched her until she closed the door behind her. And for the life of him, he couldn't explain the hollow feeling in his chest.

# Chapter Seven

"Two scoops of strawberry with chocolate sprinkles on top coming right up, Matthew." Heart heavy, Jessie concentrated on scooping ice cream into a cone for the earnest twelve-year-old. She'd set up shop on a picnic table in the church yard. Treating volunteers to ice cream was her contribution to the late-afternoon project to spruce up the church grounds since she couldn't physically handle the heavy work.

She stifled a yawn. She'd had very little sleep since Peter asked her Sunday night to move to Madison. She'd had no idea he was thinking about taking such an active role in Jake's life. And the sheer audacity of the man unnerved her. Had he really expected her to completely change her life to accommodate him? How could he think she'd just pull up stakes and move away from everybody and everything that kept her life on track? But she also felt a measure of relief that he wasn't trying to take Jake totally away from her.

Unfortunately, she could have been a little more diplomatic. What had she been thinking to chop off communication between them just before he left? She hadn't heard a word in four days, and the fact that she had no

idea what he was planning to do about Jake worried her.
She handed the double-decker cone across the table.
"Here you go."

"Thank you." Matthew scooched up his glasses on
his nose and carefully took the cone from her. "We're
all done helping Pastor Nick spread mulch."

Jessie attempted a smile. "The church will look beautiful all summer."

He nodded, his gaze riveted on his ice cream.

"Please remind the other workers to come and get
ice-cream cones when they finish their jobs."

He grinned. "I won't have to remind them when they
see mine."

"Good point."

"That's one impressive ice cream cone, Matthew."
Peeling off leather work gloves, Will strode to the table.
"You better get busy eating before it melts."

"Yeah. See ya." Matthew hurried away.

Will smiled. "Digging up those flower beds seems to
have given me a powerful taste for chocolate almonds,
Jess."

"Three scoops? Chocolate waffle cone?"

"Sounds decadent enough."

Jessie grasped a cone and stacked scoops of ice
cream.

Will glanced around as if to make sure they were
alone. "The prodigal father returning this weekend?"

Jessie frowned. "I haven't heard a word."

"What's he planning to do?"

"I don't know." She handed Will the ice cream. "He
asked me and Jake to move to Madison."

"Sounds like he's serious about being a dad. What
did you say?"

She gave him a narrow look. "What do you think I said?"

"So what now?"

"That's what worries me." She looked up as Maggie approached the table with her volunteer landscape crew in tow.

"Anything new?" Maggie asked.

Jessie shook her head.

"Hi, Jess." Mitch Miller strode to the table. "Matthew told us to get ice cream before we leave."

"Get in line, Mitch," somebody in the back of the line said.

Everybody laughed.

"Oops." Mitch rolled his eyes and moved to the end of the line.

Jessie concentrated on special requests and scooping ice cream until the line dwindled and the volunteers drifted toward their cars. Maggie, Will and Pastor Nick stayed behind to help Jessie clean up. When everything was packed in coolers and boxes, they all carried them toward the parking lot.

Lugging a cooler, Pastor Nick fell in beside Jessie. "Your treat was a big hit. Thank you."

"My pleasure. The church grounds look great."

"Yes, they do. Jessie, your dad is concerned about you. He told me about the situation with Jake's father. If you ever need to talk, you know my door is open."

"Thank you." She wished her dad hadn't shared her situation with Pastor Nick. She hated being the person everybody worried about. At least the pastor didn't feel compelled to pry. What good would talking about the situation do, anyway? The last thing she needed was to cry in front of anybody but God. She opened the van's back door and stepped aside for Pastor Nick and Will to place the coolers inside.

Jessie slammed the door. "Thanks everybody."

"No problem." Pastor Nick slapped Will on the shoulder. "I need to talk to you about church camp."

"All right." Will walked back to the church with the pastor.

"Still no news from Madison?" Maggie asked.

Jessie squinted, struggling to keep her emotions in check. Crying on Maggie's shoulder wouldn't help any more than talking to Pastor Nick.

"Maybe the less you hear from him, the better," Maggie said.

"I don't know." Jessie frowned. "If I don't know what he's planning, I can't influence his decisions."

"I see what you mean."

"I don't know why he hasn't called to find out how Jake is doing."

"It's only been a few days. Besides, he knows Jake's fine, Jess. If he wasn't, you'd let him know." Maggie brightened. "Why don't you give him a call?"

Shaking his head, Peter snapped his cell phone shut and laid it beside his laptop, which was perched on the minuscule desk in his dingy living room. Although he'd liked hearing Jessie's voice, her call had started out vague and gone nowhere fast. He'd told her the DNA test confirmed he was Jake's father, the result they'd both expected. It couldn't be clearer that neither of them had a satisfactory solution to their situation with Jake.

He focused on one of the pictures he'd downloaded from Jessie's camera Sunday. Poised to go down the slide with Jake, Peter looked like a giant next to the little guy. Good thing Jessie had reined him in on the underducks.

He thought about her stalking off last Sunday night after she'd refused to even think about moving to Madison with Jake. Had she called to bridge the gulf her hasty exit had left between them? It wouldn't surprise him. She was an amazing woman in spite of her stubborn streak.

He smiled at the picture he'd taken of her and Jake nuzzling noses. Too bad he couldn't bottle all that love they exuded and bring it home with him. He'd had a lot of fun with her and Jake at the park and, afterward, when they'd gone for ice cream. Simple pleasures he'd never had time for.

He scrolled to the next photo, the one of the three of them that the woman in the park had taken. He gazed into Jessie's crystal-blue eyes, her smile not quite masking the sadness lurking behind it. She'd opened up a little that afternoon, then dropped a curtain between them and hid from him again.

What had pulled her away? He didn't know much about women, but somehow, he'd bet there was more to her sadness than her injuries…or even her sister's death.

He liked her. Probably a good thing considering she'd be in his life for a long time because of Jake. Actually, it was more than simple like. The more he got to know her, the more fascinating he found her. She was soft and feminine and nurturing. And that vulnerable thing she had going touched him deeply. He loved her easy way with people, too, but he had the feeling she didn't open up to many.

Looking into Jake's brown eyes, he reached to touch the boy's animated face, momentarily surprised by the cold, unyielding surface of the screen. Not at all the feel of Jake's little face under his touch.

Remembering the weight of his son in his arms, he ached to hold him again. To hear his squeals of laughter. To smell his salty-sweet scent. He'd never known what real loneliness was before knowing Jake.

And he didn't like it one bit.

Sure, he'd known his personal life was empty. But he'd found purpose and enough satisfaction in his work to fortify him. Now, that didn't seem enough. He could see how empty he'd been inside. And he was making some changes.

He'd delegated parts of his workload to colleagues and gotten the process rolling to hire an assistant to pick up the overtime hours he'd been donating nights and weekends. He'd applied for grants to cover some of the additional expenses, and he'd take a pay cut if need be.

As for Jake…after talking to Jessie, it looked as if Peter needed to figure out a solution that would work for all of them.

Late Friday morning, Peter picked up the phone on his desk after ending his interview with the final babysitter candidate. The first four had fallen short, but Kelly Templeton met every criteria he could hope for. Well, she wasn't Jessie, of course. But she'd be perfect for the days he'd have to go into the lab when Jake stayed with him. Of course, he'd need to transition him gradually. And he'd need Jessie's help with that. But she'd surely see that Jake staying with him a week or two every month would be a good compromise that would work for all of them. Wouldn't she?

And Kelly Templeton seemed to fit the bill perfectly

for a part-time babysitter. She said she loved kids, was young and energetic enough to keep up with an active toddler, knew CPR and was taking child development courses at the technical college.

A few calls to references she'd listed on her application confirmed his opinion. With every glowing report, he listened for a giveaway hesitation or negative tone that would indicate a reservation about her, but he heard enthusiasm in every voice. Several people even offered anecdotes to prove Ms. Templeton went well beyond her duty.

Still, an uneasy feeling tempered his excitement. Even if she would be part-time, hiring the right babysitter was a huge decision. Crucial to Jake's well-being. Given his inexperience with little kids, he needed Jessie's input. Maybe she'd spot something he'd missed.

He left his office to keep an appointment with a Realtor to look at condos closer to the lab. He didn't want to end up stuck in traffic on evenings when he could be playing with his son.

Anyway, his dingy, one-bedroom, furnished apartment had been a temporary address when he'd rented it—nine years ago. He needed a larger place with bedrooms for himself, his son and for Jessie or her parents to stay with Jake as often as they liked when Jake was here.

By two o'clock, he'd signed on the dotted line for a great condo, picked up the new Chrysler SUV he'd traded for his MG earlier in the week and was on the highway headed for Noah's Crossing.

After enjoying his MG's ability to turn on a dime, the Chrysler felt like he was steering a bus. But it had enough room to transport whatever Jake might need, and it was a nice safe vehicle, complete with a backseat for Jake's car seat. Plus it had a screen that popped down for Jake to watch the DVDs Peter had picked out at the mega toy store where he'd bought the car seat. He figured the DVD player was just the thing for trips to Noah's Crossing when he drove Jake back and forth to Jessie's.

There was still the babysitter question to settle, of course. He was anxious to bring Jessie and Jake to Madison to see if the babysitter measured up to Jessie's standards.

The drive seemed to take forever. He couldn't wait to see Jake. And he couldn't deny he was a little anxious about working out an arrangement with Jessie, but of course, she knew as well as he did one had to be worked out between them. As for her coming to Madison to meet Kelly Templeton, he was sure Jessie would be concerned about who would care for Jake when Peter had to be at the lab.

Finally, he arrived at the Chandlers, only to have Jessie's dad inform him Jessie had taken Jake to the lake to cool off after supper. So Peter followed her dad's directions to Rainbow Lake a couple miles east of town.

After parking the SUV, he dodged towels and families on the beach, the smell of lake heavy in the humid air. The carefree shouts of children rang in his ears as he looked for Jessie and his son. Scanning the water, he spotted them a few yards out.

Jessie lifted Jake in the air, then scooped him into the water to the boy's shrieks of delight. Her joyful laughter rode the slight breeze along with the flying water.

Anxiety drained away and energy poured through Peter's body. Feeling as if he'd come home after a lifetime of absence, he sank to the sand and watched them, unable and unwilling to do anything else.

Jessie handed Jake to the petite redhead beside her, then immersed herself in the lake. When she bounced back up in a spray of water, the little guy squealed with laughter.

Peter laughed, too, in spite of the lump in his throat. His son and his mother…he could watch them all day.

After swimming a couple laps, Jessie waded to shallow water with her friend, who set Jake on his feet.

Jake plopped down and began splashing like he did in the bathtub.

Laughing, Jessie backed away from the splashes, her deep-blue bathing suit clinging to her womanly curves like a second skin.

She was…amazing.

Peter glanced around. Probably most of the men on the beach were watching her—a thought that gave him a fiercely protective shot of adrenaline. He climbed to his feet and strode to the water's edge. "Jessie."

She looked up. "Peter?" Obviously, she hadn't expected to see him.

The boy peered in Peter's direction. "Pedo!" Jake tried to scramble to his feet. With Jessie's help, he made it up and ran full-tilt for the shore.

Laughing, Peter swooped him in the air, life jacket and all. Water flew everywhere. Hugging the dripping boy, he drew in the smell of him. "I've missed you so much."

Jake laughed.

"Did you miss me, Jake?" Why he asked, he didn't know. Nobody had ever told him they'd missed him. Or if they had, it had never been this important to him. He held his son at arm's length and gave him a once-over. "I swear you've grown since I saw you."

He looked at Jessie. He could feel the coolness of her

from the lake water. Water from her hair ran in rivulets over her silky shoulders and chest. Light seemed to sparkle in her eyes. She was so lovely, he had trouble breathing.

"Off." Jake tugged at his red life vest.

Peter set him down.

Jessie bent over the boy, whipped off the vest and straightened. She turned to a woman beside her. "Maggie, this is Peter Sheridan. Peter, Maggie Maguire."

He smiled. "Nice to meet you, Maggie."

The attractive redhead with snapping brown eyes gave him a less than friendly nod, then looked to Jessie. "I'm heading home, Jess. Unless you want me to stay." She threw a wary look Peter's way.

What was that about?

"I'll call you later," Jessie said, her eyes on Peter.

"Nice meeting you," Peter offered politely.

Maggie lifted an eyebrow, turned and walked away.

Downright chilly. Apparently, Jessie hadn't sung his praises to her friend. Under the circumstances, he shouldn't be surprised. Or disappointed. But somehow, he was.

"I didn't know you were coming this weekend," Jessie said.

"I hope that's not a problem."

"I'd appreciate it if you'd let me know in advance when you plan to stop by."

"Duly noted." Not the best start. But he couldn't let it discourage him. "Can we walk somewhere quieter so we can talk?"

She gave him a small frown. "There's the bike path. But Jake and I need to get some shoes first." She led the way to her beach bag and handed Peter a pair of tiny sandals.

He wanted to grasp her hand but thought better of the idea. While he struggled to fit the sandals on his son's small, wet, sandy, wiggly feet, Jessie tied a white towel around her waist and slipped into her own sandals. Then she guided the way to a wooded bike path. They strolled away from the beach, Jake stopping to pick up stones and twigs along the way.

Peter tamped down his nervousness. "I missed Jake like crazy."

Jessie gave him a pinched look.

He wished he knew what she was thinking. Or maybe it was better that he didn't. "Scott used to tell me to get a life. He said research alone didn't cut it. But I never understood what he meant before I met Jake. The little guy has a way of putting things in perspective."

"Yes."

Peter blew out a breath. At least she'd agreed with him. Maybe telling her all he'd accomplished would be the best way to ease into his reasons for being here. "I've made some changes in my life in the past week. I bought a great condo close to the lab with lots of windows and natural light. Very unlike the dingy little furnished place I live in now."

"Really." She kept her eyes on Jake.

"The condo doesn't come with furniture though, so I have lots of shopping to do."

"Sounds exciting."

Unfortunately, she didn't sound or look excited—or even interested, for that matter. He needed to get to the point. "I'd like the place to be warm and comfortable— a real home. I could use your help with that. Especially with Jake's room."

Stopping dead, she whirled on him. "Jake's room?"

He sure had her attention now but not in a good way. "For when he stays with me."

"When he stays with you." She narrowed her eyes. "When he gets older?"

"As soon as I can pull everything together, I'd like to begin transitioning him."

*"Transitioning him?"* Propping her hands on her hips, she glowered at him as if she couldn't stomach what she saw.

He'd known it wouldn't be easy, hadn't he? He drew himself to his full height. "I want to get him used to living with me a week or two at a time. Of course, we need to work out an arrangement that works for both of us."

Taking a step closer, she jabbed her finger into his chest. "You promised you'd put Jake's needs first."

He stood his ground. "That's what I'm doing. I'm re-organizing my life to include him."

"But he has a family. I'm his mother."

"I know that." She was so focused on her anger, she didn't seem to get that he wasn't threatening her relationship with Jake. He needed to reassure her. "I'll never come between you and Jake, Jessie. The condo has plenty of room, even an extra bedroom for you or your parents to stay as much as you like when he's with me."

She shut her eyes. "My parents and I can *visit* him?" she whispered.

He tried to ignore the accusation in her tone. He needed to make her see the entire picture. "You can stay with him anytime he's with me. Anytime you want. For as long as you want."

She pressed her hand to her forehead. "What do you think you're doing?"

He swallowed. "I'm doing my best to figure out a way to be Jake's father. And I think I've found a well-qualified caretaker for when I have to work. I think you'll like her."

She stiffened. "A *nanny?* You hired a *nanny?*"

"No." His gut twisted. This was going from bad to worse, and he didn't know how to stop it. "She's a babysitter. And I want your input before I hire her. I'd like to drive you and Jake down to meet her as soon as possible."

She took a step back. "You were scheming to separate us all along?"

"What? No. I was never scheming." Struggling to get a foothold in the quicksand he'd managed to stumble into, he reached out to touch her arm.

She jerked away.

He dropped his hand to his side. "I'm trying to work out a compromise. I told you I don't want my son growing up without his father like I did. I think the best way to do that is to have him live with me part of the time, don't you?"

"No. He's too young to be shifted back and forth between us. If you cared about him, you'd see that." Her words were clipped, her tone seething.

"Jessie—"

"Don't 'Jessie' me. Nothing you have to say interests me now that I know how underhanded you really are."

Flinching, he raised his hand in front of him to try to calm her down.

"How could I have been so wrong about you? How could I have ever believed Jake was lucky to have you for a daddy?"

She'd believed that?

"Mama mad?" Jake peered up at her, eyes wide.

"Yes, Mama's mad, sweetie."

The little guy scowled up at Peter. "Bad Pedo."

Pain stabbed his chest. He dragged in a breath and tried to figure out where things had gone so wrong and what to do about it.

Jessie scooped Jake up and took a step closer to Peter, her eyes dark with anger. "Your nanny can rot for all I care. And so can your condo. If you think I'll *ever* hand him over to you, you don't know me at all." Turning, she strode away without a backward glance.

Peter stood rooted to the spot, his heart thudding so hard against his ribs, its pounding muffled everything else. The anxiety he'd been fighting crashed over him in waves. He felt as if he were drowning in them.

# Chapter Eight

Still in her swimsuit, Jessie strode up the driveway, hugging Jake to her for all she was worth. She never wanted to see Peter Sheridan again as long as she lived.

Jake patted her face assuringly.

She kissed his forehead. She hated upsetting Jake. She'd done her best to calm down ever since she'd left Peter at the lake, but she just couldn't get past how completely he'd fooled her.

*Why did you bring Peter into our lives, God?* she asked angrily. *I even began to trust him.*

Look where that had gotten her. She'd taught Jake to trust him, too. Stupid. No wonder she hadn't heard from Peter. He'd been plotting to take Jake away all along. And she'd played right into his hands.

"See Papa?"

"Yes, honey. Papa will make Mama feel better." Too bad her problems had been too big for a very long time for her dad to chase them away with a pat on the head or a kiss on the cheek.

Spotting him on the patio working, tears she'd been too angry to let fall spilled over and ran down her face.

She swiped at them. Jake didn't need to see her cry on top of everything else. She needed to bathe him and get him into bed before she let herself fall apart.

Her dad looked up, his smile fading. "What's wrong, Jess?"

She pressed her fingers to her lips to stifle a sob.

Jake lunged for his grandfather, spreading his arms to be held.

He took him, his eyes still on Jessie.

"Pedo bad." Jake stuck out his bottom lip.

Dad hugged Jake to him and frowned at Jessie. "What happened?"

Stifling another sob, Jessie shook her head and pointed at Jake.

"Jake, your toys have been waiting for you in the sandbox. Think you should tell them hello?"

Jake's little face brightened. "Down, Papa."

Jessie's dad helped him slide to the ground.

Jake ran across the yard to the sandbox, climbed in and plopped in the sand, jabbering to his toys.

Her father stood and opened his arms.

Stepping into them, Jessie blubbered against his shoulder as if her heart would break.

He patted her back and let her cry.

She glanced at Jake. Hopefully, he was too absorbed with his toys to notice her crying jag. When she was able to stop the tears, she reached to grab tissues from the box on the nearby table and set about mopping her face and blowing her nose.

"What happened?" Dad asked. "Peter was in a good mood when I sent him to the lake to find you and Jake."

"I'll just bet he was. He thought he had everything wrapped up in a neat little package." Glancing at Jake, she lowered her voice even further. "I tried to give Peter the benefit of the doubt, and he thought he had me totally wrapped around his little finger. The man is insufferable, Dad. He even had the nerve to ask for my input on hiring a...a...*nanny*."

A new surge of tears wound their way down her cheeks. She dabbed at them. "He bought a new condo. He's been making plans to take Jake to live with him. As soon as we can transition him." She shook her head. "*Transition* him? Over my dead body. I've been naive and stupid to think he would do what was best for Jake."

"What did you tell him?"

"That I'd never hand Jake over to him. Period."

Dad frowned. "Do you think he'll take you to court?"

"Court?" Fear clutched her. She'd been so angry and upset, she hadn't considered Peter could fight for custody and probably win. How could she protect Jake then? She pressed her palm to her forehead. "I don't know," she whispered.

"When you told him you wouldn't hand Jake over, how did he react?"

"She didn't give me a chance to react." Peter strode from the driveway as if he had a right to be here.

How arrogant could the man be to show up after what he'd done? Jessie's gaze darted to Jake.

Jake looked up, obviously recognizing Peter's voice.

Poor little boy. He'd already had more emotional upheaval tonight than he should be expected to handle. She strode to the sandbox, picked him up and hurried into the house.

\* \* \*

"Jessie," Peter hollered. How could he make her understand if she kept running away from him? He strode after her.

"Let her go, Peter." Jessie's dad used an authoritative tone Peter hadn't heard before.

Stopping mid-stride, he turned to him. "I need to talk to her."

Max shook his head. "Jake doesn't need to hear any more."

Peter blew out a breath. "You're right."

"Jess is too upset to listen right now, anyway."

"But I need to make her understand."

Jessie's dad gave him a grim look. "You've made arrangements to take Jake to live with you?"

"Part of the time."

Max scowled. "Do you really expect her to understand *that?*"

Peter stared at the ground. "Well, yes. I wasn't trying to take him away from her. I hoped we could put our heads together and figure out an arrangement that will work for all of us. I told her I'll never keep Jake from her. Or from you and your wife, either. My new condo has an extra bedroom for you all whenever you want."

"Jess can *visit* Jake?" Max shook his head, a deep frown furrowing his brow. "What were you thinking?"

Peter blew out a breath. "I'm thinking of Jake. I never knew my own parents. I don't want to do that to my son."

"But Jess is his mother."

Peter swallowed. "I know. But I'm also his father."

"Do you know what a mother is?" Max gave him a sour look. "Because Jake knows."

Peter sighed. "I don't want to change their relationship, Max."

"It sounds like you do want to change it. Are you planning to take Jess to court? Because that's what it will take, you know."

Peter met the man's direct gaze. Scott had asked him how far he'd be willing to go to have Jake with him. It looked like time to figure that out. "A legal battle would hurt everybody involved, and alienating Jessie and you would only make things harder for Jake. Plus I'd hate myself for doing it. So no, I won't go to court."

Jessie's father let out a breath. "Well, thank God for that. But you hired a nanny?"

"She's a babysitter. And I didn't hire her. Not without Jessie's input."

Max shook his head again. "I think she's given her input on that idea."

Peter glanced at the house. Was Jessie getting Jake ready for bed? He ached to be part of that ritual again. He shifted his feet, ready to walk in and claim his rightful place. "I need to make her understand. We need to work this out."

"*You* don't understand, Peter."

Peter dragged in a breath.

"Your wanting to be part of Jake's life is commendable, but he has a mother who's been with him since birth. He's part of a family. The family he's known since day one. A family that thrives on daily routine. That's how family members become connected enough to understand each other on a deep level. Think about it. Your son trusts Jess to always be there no matter what happens."

"I know. Am I wrong for wanting that kind of relationship with Jake, too?"

"No. You're not wrong, but it takes time to build trust like that. How much do you think Jake will trust you if you take him away from his mother?"

Peter felt like he'd been sucker punched.

"He's a little boy, Peter. He's not a lab experiment you can shift around or manipulate at your will or convenience."

He stared at the older man. "That's what you think I'm doing?"

"Maybe not intentionally." Max's gaze was steady, his voice unyielding. "But yes, I think that's what you're doing."

Peter tried to wrap his mind around the cold, controlling man Jessie's dad described. Was he that kind of man? He sure hoped not. "Is that what Jessie thinks?"

"She loves Jake, and she knows what you're planning will hurt him. Do you know your son well enough to know what will hurt him? Or to know what's best for him?" Max shook his head. "I don't think so. If you did, you'd see your plans aren't for him. They're for yourself."

Peter's arguments died on his lips. Was Max right? Was he thinking of himself? Of his own lonely childhood?

Jake's childhood was nothing like his had been. Jake had Jessie. And her parents. And a home filled with love. His son had a family and the deep understanding and communication Peter never had. What kind of father would take that away?

With a sinking feeling, he clawed his fingers through his hair. "But he needs to know I love him and want him in my life."

"Yes, he does. You can show him that by spending time with him whenever you can."

No Jake to hurry home to? To read stories to or tuck into bed? To fill his new condo with laughter and love? He ached inside. He hadn't realized how much he was looking forward to having the little guy in his life on a regular basis.

But would Jake laugh without Jessie? And if he took his son from his mother, would he ever trust Peter again? He blew out a breath. "Seeing him on weekends will be better than nothing."

"It's the right thing for Jake, Peter."

His stomach twisted. Had he even thought about Jake's feelings when he was so busy making plans? Or only his own? He glanced at the house. "I need to tell Jessie."

"Not so fast. You think she's going to trust you around Jake after what you pulled? I'll tell her you won't sue for custody. That's what she's most worried about."

Peter dragged in a breath, remembering her reaction to his plans. *How could I have ever believed Jake was lucky to have you for a daddy?* He could still hear the accusation in her voice, see the distrust in her eyes. He hadn't considered her feelings either, had he? "What can I do to fix this, Max?"

"I think you're going to have to give her a little time. Go home, let her calm down while you figure out how you began to win her trust in the first place. Then go from there."

Peter stared at the older man. He didn't know why Jessie had decided to trust him. Or when she'd begun to think Jake was lucky to have him for a dad. Was it that night when she'd let him share Jake's bath and defended him to his son after he'd let the little guy fall?

Probably not. Why would she trust him after he'd failed to keep Jake safe?

Maybe when she'd coached him through Jake's bedtime ritual? Or that day in the park when she'd taken pictures and offered to share those she already had of Jake?

He'd accepted her acts of kindness as if they were his due. He scrubbed his hands over his face. How had he been so blind?

She'd allowed him into her and Jake's life. She'd let him see their mysterious connection up close and personal. He'd been warmed by it. And what had he done? He'd rejected being part of the life she'd built for Jake and pursued his own interests.

*That's* how he'd lost her trust.

Not out of malice, as she probably suspected. Out of ignorance. Which was, obviously, just as deadly.

The problem was he didn't have a clue how to win her trust again. All he knew was he needed to find a way.


Jessie sat on her bed, legs folded to support her laptop. A whole week had ground slowly past without so much as a word from Peter. If he hadn't promised her father he wouldn't sue for custody, she'd be a total basket case.

Putting off another night of tossing and turning, she scrolled through several email subject lines. At a blank subject, she checked the address. Jakesdad. Drawing a breath, she paused her finger over the delete icon.

What could he possibly think he had to say to her now? Nothing that would help her sleep. Her emotions had been all over the place ever since she met the man. Reading his email would confuse her more than she already was. She pushed Delete and opened an email from her cousin, Mary, full of excited plans about her upcoming wedding.

Jessie read the rest of her mail, answering the ones that called for a reply. About to turn off her laptop, she hesitated. How well would she sleep if she *didn't* read Peter's email?

Was not knowing what he said even worse than knowing? Making a face, she scrolled to Recently Deleted. Peter's mail was the only one in the list. She stared at it for several seconds, then clicked it open and read.

Dear Jessie,
I was wrong to think I could give Jake what he needs.
Your dad helped me see you and Jake are a family. I didn't get that before. Taking him away from you would be a mistake that would hurt him possibly for the rest of his life.
Another thing I understand now is that being a dad isn't about me. At least, it shouldn't be. It's about what's best for our son. I want to add to the terrific life you've made for him…not make it less.
Please forgive me, Jessie. For making you think you can't trust me. I've figured out I didn't deserve your trust. But I hope you can find it in your heart to give me another chance. I'll do whatever it takes.
And I promise to spend the rest of my life trying to earn the privilege of being Jake's dad.
Peter

She pressed her fingers to her lips to hold back the onslaught of emotions threatening to overwhelm her. How could she sleep after reading a letter like that?

*But how do I know if he means what he says? If I let him get close to Jake, will he try to take him away again?*

Or was it like her father had said? Peter hadn't understood because he'd never had a family? Had he really thought he could rip Jake away and become his family, just like that?

She couldn't begin to imagine what it would have been like for him growing up without parents and relatives. Her heart ached thinking how lonely and afraid a little boy would be never knowing he was loved unconditionally. The way her parents loved Clarissa and her.

The way she loved Jake.

She had to protect her little boy and do what was best for him, no matter what. Knowing his daddy cared about him would be best for him, wouldn't it? But would she be protecting Jake if she trusted Peter after what he'd tried to do? *Oh, God, what if I make a mistake that hurts Jake?*

Nothing could change that Peter was Jake's daddy. Or that Jake deserved and needed him. How could she claim to love her son unless she forgave his father and gave him a second chance?

She hit Reply and stared at the blinking cursor for who knew how long. But words just wouldn't come. Finally, she switched off her laptop and breathed a heavy sigh. It looked like another sleepless night lay in wait.

Her gaze rested on the phone, then the clock. It was 1:00 a.m. already? Too late to call Peter. Besides, what would she say? She could only hope the right words would come to her when she heard his voice.

Before she could change her mind, she grasped her little directory and found the cell-phone number he'd given her in case of emergency. If she woke him, too bad. Her own sleep deprivation was reaching the emergency stage, wasn't it? She punched in his number. The phone rang three times, four…

"Sheridan."

His deep voice sent a ripple along her nerves. She almost hung up but managed to stop herself. "Peter?"

"Jessie?"

He recognized her voice? Unprepared for the warm flood of emotion, she scooped her hair off her neck.

"Is Jake okay?"

She heard the alarm in his tone. "He's fine. I'm sorry if I woke you."

"I wasn't asleep."

Did he have trouble sleeping, too? "I read your email."

A pause. "I mean every word, Jessie." He sounded sincere enough.

She swallowed around a lump in her throat. "I hope so."

"And I'm so sorry."

She bit her lip. "I won't let you hurt Jake," she warned.

"I know. You were right to protect him."

She sniffed, not knowing what to say. Words weren't coming much easier on the phone than when she'd tried to write to him. "I'm sure you'd like to see him."

"Very much. When?" he said in a rush.

She wasn't ready for him. "This weekend won't work. When I'm not at the diner, Jake and I will be picking strawberries Saturday. And we have a church fundraiser Sunday."

"Okay." He sounded disappointed.

She swallowed guiltily. "The berries are ripening too fast for my aunt and uncle to keep up, so we're all helping out whenever we can." True, but a lame excuse nonetheless.

"Will next weekend work?"

Could she make him wait another whole week to see Jake? Of course she could.

No. She couldn't.

He was being real. The fear and defeat on his face when Jake fell was real. So was the laughter in his eyes when he played with his son. And his rusty monotone singing "Happy Birthday" along with Jake's sweet hum wasn't an act, any more than his dedication to his research, his loyalty to his friend Scott or his determination to be the father to Jake that Peter never had.

How could she make him wait another week? He was sacrificing having his son live with him, wasn't he? She had to compromise, too. "You can come out to my aunt and uncle's place Saturday to play with Jake if you like."

"Tomorrow? I'll be there with bells on," he said hoarsely.

Swiping at a pesky tear winding its way down her cheek, she gave him directions to her aunt and uncle's farm.

"Jessie…"

"Yes."

"Thank you."

She forced her trembling hand to set the phone in its cradle, then stared at it as if it were a living thing. Hearing his voice, his words, she was sure he meant what he said in his email.

It was the ache in her heart that worried her. That and the way she was suddenly looking forward to seeing him far too much.

# *Chapter Nine*

A yellow Labrador retriever loudly welcomed Peter to Jessie's aunt and uncle's strawberry patch—a misnomer if he'd ever seen one. Anybody but Jessie's family would call the patch a field. He'd never seen so many strawberries. And the patch/field was scattered with people picking the berries. Jessie's parents gave him friendly waves. He returned them, glad they seemed okay with him being here.

But it didn't take him long to hone in on a rainbow-striped umbrella. In its shade, a small boy played with trucks in the dirt. And near him, his mother picked strawberries under a wide straw hat.

The sensation of coming home after a long absence hit him just as it had that day at the beach. He'd missed his son even more than he'd realized. And no denying, he'd missed Jessie, too. Feeling like his chest might explode, he strode for them as fast as he could cover ground.

She sat in the dirt, her red-stained fingers deftly plucking berries. The hat shaded her face, cutoffs exposed her long legs and a blue tank top with seahorses all over it bared her creamy shoulders. He couldn't take his gaze from her.

She looked up, her eyes going wide when she saw him, almost as if she was as glad to see him as he was to see her. But she shuttered her gaze just as quickly. "Look, Jake. Peter's here."

No mistaking the reserve in her voice. Obviously, the invitation to the strawberry field didn't mean she trusted him automatically. He needed to watch his step. He had to show her that his son was his first priority, that he finally got it. And that he'd learned a lesson he'd never forget. Dragging his gaze away, he ducked under the umbrella and dropped to his knees beside the boy. "Hi, Jake."

Jake squinted at him. "Truck."

"I see it. Are you having fun?"

"Mommy." He pointed at Jessie.

Peter raised his hand in greeting. "Hi, Mommy."

Jessie raised her hand, but looked at Jake with concern. "Peter drove all this way to play with you. Will you share your trucks with him?"

"No." Jake's bottom lip puckered in a pout. "Mommy mad."

Wow. The little guy remembered that day at the beach? Or had he picked up on the wariness in her voice today?

"No, sweetie. Mommy's not mad anymore." She shot a fake smile Peter's way. "We're friends, aren't we, Peter?"

Friends? The way he felt when he first saw her somehow made friends seem…inadequate. He'd missed her more than he'd miss merely a friend. But keeping it real, he gave her a nod. "Friends."

Jake studied Peter, then reached for the blue semi and handed it to him. "Pedo play?"

"I'd love to play with you, Jake." He gave Jessie a thumbs-up.

She went back to picking berries, still wearing her worried look.

Peter settled in to play trucks with Jake until the little guy sacked out in the dirt mid-haul. Watching the boy sleep, the rise of his tummy as he breathed in and out, Peter's throat closed. Being a father was an amazing thing. Full of awe and wonder but tempered with so much fear of not measuring up. He looked to Jessie. "Looks like my pal is done playing for now."

"He's all worn out. Will you carry him over there?" She pointed to a truck with a small wagon attached. "I spread a blanket under that big tree for his nap."

"Will he wake up if I move him?"

"No, he's a sound sleeper. He'll be out for a couple hours."

Gathering Jake's warm little body in his arms, Peter stood and carried him to the giant bur oak Jessie had pointed out. He bent and carefully laid the boy on the black-and-red-plaid blanket. Jake didn't stir. Looked like he was out for the duration, just like Jessie said. Peter walked away, grabbed an empty pail from a stack beside the truck and strode back to Jessie.

Her gaze stayed riveted on the berries under her flying fingers.

He watched, mesmerized. She looked like a woman in an ad for strawberries. Problem was, he wanted to remove her hat, unfasten her ponytail and sift her hair through his fingers to see if it was as silky as it looked.

She glanced up at him. "Do I have strawberries on my face?"

He scrutinized her flawless face. "Not that I can see."

"Then why the grin?"

Uh-oh. "Uh, I was thinking you should model for the strawberry industry."

She rolled her eyes. "Right. Modeling would be right up my alley," she said sarcastically.

"Too much sitting around for you?"

"That's one of a million things, including the fact that I weigh twice as much as any model."

She didn't have an extra ounce anywhere that he could see. "You hide it well," he teased.

She gave him a look laced with surprise, then dropped her gaze to the berries again.

*Watch it, Sheridan.* Either he'd embarrassed her or she thought teasing her was being too familiar. Either way, he needed to remember he was treading on thin ice. Letting her take the lead might be a good idea. He staked out a place near her, dropped to his knees and concentrated on picking strawberries. Slowly. All thumbs.

Her fresh lemon scent drifted on the breeze and mixed with the sweet perfume of the berries. All he heard was the murmur of other workers, the twittering of birds and an occasional drone of an insect or bee.

Not a computer or lab coat in sight. He'd never been more out of his element. But gone was the emptiness he'd felt as he knocked around in that bare condo of his. How could he feel that empty? For the moment, his son was nearby. And so was Jessie.

He wouldn't have blamed Jessie if she'd made him wait to see Jake. But she hadn't. Wary or not, she had a far more generous spirit than he deserved. Noting how slowly berries were piling up in his bucket, he concentrated on picking them faster.

"How is your friend Scott?" Jessie's soft voice broke into Peter's thoughts.

He noticed she'd begun filling another pail. She picked berries like a pro. But then, what wasn't she good at? "Earlier this week, his doctors started giving him the drug our lab developed."

"That's wonderful. I hope it works better than you ever anticipated."

"I appreciate that. I'll pass your words on to Scott." No offer to pray for them this time. Apparently, she'd figured out he'd felt uncomfortable that day in the van. Today, he'd know enough to thank her. And he'd mean it, too.

"Did you cancel the nanny?"

He was surprised by her question. It appeared she wasn't going to skirt the difficult issues. "Sitter. And I never hired her, Jessie. I wanted your input before doing that."

She bit her lip. "What about the condo? Do you plan to sell it?"

"The condo? No. I moved in yesterday. If you call sleeping on the great-room floor in a sleeping bag moving in. But I don't know the first thing about what to put in the place." Oh. Hadn't he asked her to help him buy furniture that day at the lake? He sure didn't want to tweak those memories.

"You need a decorator."

"I don't want it decorated. I want it to feel comfortable. You know, like a home."

"A home for Jake?" Her tone held a warning.

"Sure, when he's old enough to stay with me for a

few days. But for now, I don't want him to get used to the idea that I'm only a visitor in his life. Do you think you can bring him to Madison for a visit some time so he can get comfortable at my place?"

She squinted. "The diner is always hectic during the tourist season."

Just how long did tourist season last? Until Labor Day? Later? He didn't think he could bear to wait months for her to free up time for him. *Careful, Sheridan. Don't push her.*

But his relationship with his son was too important to let this drop. "Is there any way you can work something out?"

"What do you want her to work out?" Suspicion in her voice, Jessie's chubby aunt Lou strode by, a pail of strawberries dangling from each hand.

Peter sighed. Lou looked ready to defend her niece. But he decided to lay out his problem anyway. "I'd like Jessie to bring Jake to Madison to visit, so he'll feel comfortable in the new condo I bought."

Aunt Lou gave Jessie a shrug. "You could use a couple days away from the diner."

A pleasant surprise. Peter wanted to give Aunt Lou a high five.

Jessie rolled her eyes her aunt's way and continued picking berries. "Never mind that I need to make a living, Aunt Lou."

"Hmph." Aunt Lou didn't sound convinced. "Peter, carry those pails to the wagon, will you? Harold and I have to get back to the house to get berries ready for the church benefit tomorrow. And we're hungry. Jess, you said you made sandwiches, right?" Aunt Lou bustled off.

"Sure did," Jessie called after her. She struggled to get up.

Peter jumped up and grasped Jessie's firm forearm to help her.

"I'm fine, thanks." Shaking him off, she climbed to her feet.

He frowned. Why wouldn't she let him help her?

She stretched her back as if she was stiff.

"Do you have a lot of pain from your accident?" he asked.

"Not much…if I keep moving." She slowly limped away.

He had the feeling she was pushing through more pain than she'd admit…maybe even to herself. Noting that her parents and most of the berry pickers had already left, he grasped the pail handles and headed to the wagon. Following Aunt Lou's example, he stashed the buckets of strawberries in the wagon with the others.

The yellow Lab who'd greeted him when he arrived lay panting in the shade of the truck, his liquid brown eyes on Peter.

"Hey, fella." Peter walked over to him, bent and patted his head. The dog licked his hand, his long tongue like silk on Peter's skin. Peter had to smile. Maybe he'd get a dog to keep him company in his big empty condo.

"Help yourselves to cold drinks and sandwiches." Jessie knelt beside the cooler, snatched a bottle of cola and held it to her neck to cool off.

Peter watched, too fascinated not to.

Using the cooler for support, she struggled to her feet and limped to check Jake.

Peter grabbed a cold bottle of water from the cooler

and strolled over to stand beside her. He grinned down at Jake sprawled on the blanket. "I don't think he's moved since I laid him down."

"He still needs his late-morning naps," Jessie said.

Peter polished off his bottle of water. A small black-and-white bird twittered in the bur oak above their heads. Peter couldn't remember ever feeling more alive.

"What do you say, Peter?"

Peter turned.

"You ready to hire on by the hour to pick strawberries?" Aunt Lou's hefty husband, Harold, moved to stand by his wife, who'd perched on a pail turned upside down. The dog lay beside her.

Peter and Jessie walked back to them. "You'd go broke if you paid me by the hour, Mr. Phillips. My big, clumsy fingers move very slowly."

The older man chuckled. "I haven't told you how low my hourly wage is, have I?"

Peter grinned.

Wheezing a deep laugh, Harold stiffly lowered himself to the ground. "Everybody calls me Harold except Louise when she's mad at me." Another deep, wheezy laugh.

Peter chuckled. Jessie's uncle was beginning to grow on him.

Bent over the cooler, Jessie handed plastic-bagged sandwiches all around. "I hope you like sliced turkey and cheese."

"Sounds good." Peter accepted the sandwich and sat down in the grass beside her to unwrap it. He took a bite of the best turkey-and-cheese sandwich he'd ever tasted. "This is great. Special sauce?"

"Yes. Glad you like it." She took a bite of her own sandwich.

He watched her chew, then realized he was staring again and looked away.

"You know, Jess…" Aunt Lou pursed her lips. "There's no reason you can't take Jake to see Peter's condo. There are enough of us to pitch in and make the diner work without you for a day or two."

Peter liked the way Aunt Lou thought.

Unfortunately, Jessie stared at the ground, obviously in no mood to entertain her aunt's suggestion.

Harold cleared his throat. "I see you aren't driving that anemic car anymore, Peter. Did you trade it in?"

Chewing, Peter nodded.

"Get tired of pouring that big body of yours in that little tin can?" he asked.

Peter swallowed the last bite. "I had more room in the MG than you might think, but it didn't have a back-seat for Jake's car seat." He looked at Jessie. "The SUV is safer, too. And it'll be better in winter."

Jessie nodded, the corners of her lips quirking as if they wanted to smile.

Interpreting her reaction as approval, Peter couldn't help a grin.

Harold cleared his throat again. "I suppose the little sports job got a lot better gas mileage than the SUV does."

Peter tore his gaze from Jessie to focus on her uncle. "Sure did. It was fun to drive, too."

"You must be hurting for fun," Aunt Lou interjected.

"I work long hours, so I take fun where I can find it."

"Like picking strawberries on your day off?" Harold gave him a wink and raised his eyebrows Jessie's way.

Had Harold picked up on Peter's attraction to Jessie? He could only hope his feelings weren't that obvious.

"Jake loves strawberries, so I wanted him to see where we get them," Jessie explained. "And Peter was kind enough to agree to play with him here." Jessie took a drink of her soda, apparently satisfied she'd set the record straight that Peter was here for Jake, not her.

And before Peter had seen her today, he would have agreed.

"Look at the little tyke, not a care in the world." Aunt Lou gazed at Jake from her perch on the pail. "Jake and Lisa's little Denise will have a grand time when she learns to walk," Lou predicted.

"Playmates are pretty important to little kids, I guess." Peter looked at Jessie.

Jessie raised an eyebrow.

Peter smiled. What was he trying to do, impress her with his knowledge about kids? Laughable.

"We'll take a couple pails of berries to the diner for you to use or freeze, Jess," her aunt interjected.

"Thank you, Aunt Lou. You know our customers love them."

"It's a good year. They'll be delicious in that fancy, strawberry-cream wedding cake you promised to bake for Mary's reception. She's so excited about it. We appreciate it."

"The cake is my wedding gift to her."

"It will be perfect. If you're in town the weekend of our daughter's wedding, you're invited, Peter."

"Thank you." Warmed by the inclusion, he glanced at Jessie. Was she okay with her aunt's invitation to share a private family wedding? He couldn't tell.

"Thanks to both of you for picking berries today. We hate to see them spoil when we can't get to them fast enough, don't we, Harold?"

Harold swallowed the last bite of his sandwich. "Yes, we do. Nice of you to pitch in."

Lou stood up. "It's time we go back to the house."

"Be right there, Lou, just as soon as I can make these creaky knees cooperate." Harold started to climb awkwardly to his feet.

Peter stood and reached to offer a hand.

Unlike Jessie, Harold used it for support. "Thanks."

Peter gave a nod.

"We'll stay and pick berries, Aunt Lou. If we wake Jake now, he'll be cranky all afternoon."

"Stay as long as you like. But you've picked enough berries. You can use a rest, Jess."

"But—"

"Please." Lou made the word sound like a command rather than request. "Peter, you keep after her to take time off and take Jake to that place of yours. And while she's there, pick her brain on how to spruce it up. She can turn anything into a warm, cozy home. If you don't believe me, make her show you that cute little apartment she's fixing up over the diner."

Jessie had an apartment? Peter looked at her. "I'd like to see it."

Jessie frowned as if she had no intention of ever showing him the place.

He dragged in a breath. *Don't get ahead of yourself, Sheridan.*

"A little trip would do you a world of good, Jess. You used to enjoy Madison. Have you even been there since you and Neil—"

"Aunt...Lou." Jessie's tone emphasized the warning in her eyes.

Neil? Who was *Neil?*

Lou pursed her lips. "Well, see you at the diner, Jess, in time to help with the supper crowd. And we'll look forward to seeing you at the church benefit tomorrow, Peter." With that, she turned, walked to the truck, climbed in and pulled the door shut behind her.

"Come on, Scout." Harold strode to the driver's side and opened the door. The dog hopped aboard. Harold got in behind the wheel and slowly drove away, the wagon full of strawberries bouncing behind them.

Jessie busied her hands with picking grass and piling it together in a neat little stack.

She seemed uneasy. Was she worried he'd ask her about her trips to Madison with Neil? He had to give it a try. "You enjoy Madison?"

She glanced at him. "It's a beautiful city with the capitol and all the lakes."

She sounded as vague as a travel advertisement. "Did you spend time on State Street?"

She nodded.

"With Neil?"

She concentrated on the grass in her fingers. "Yes. With Neil."

She said his name with far too much regard. "Does he live in Madison?"

"No. California."

"California." Much better. "Then I suppose you don't see him often?"

With a brush of her hand, she scattered the grass she'd so carefully piled together. "It's been two years."

Two years. He liked the sound of that. But it was obvious Jessie didn't. "What happened two years ago?"

"What happened two years ago?" She sighed. "We ended our engagement."

Wow. She'd been engaged? Was her broken engagement the reason behind the sadness in her eyes? He should let the whole thing drop, but the seriousness of her tone wouldn't let him. "Are you still in love with him?"

"Of course not," she said too quickly.

Peter swallowed hard. "What happened?"

She shook her head.

He willed himself not to push his luck. Continuing his line of questioning would only alienate her. He needed to win her trust, not demand answers she wasn't willing to give.

Anyway, how much more did he need to hear to know she was hurting over a failed relationship? Neil must be pretty special if she was engaged to marry him.

And she was his son's mother, that's all. Well, not all. She was a beautiful, loving woman, and he was attracted to her. No mystery there.

He dragged in a deep breath. With a chaser of apprehension. He'd never known a woman like Jessie. Oh, he worked with strong, capable, beautiful women like she was. But Jessie had a softness about her and a fresh glow that enticed him to look at things with new eyes. Small things like reading his son a book or picking strawberries on a sunny day took on an importance all their own.

What would it take to be the kind of guy a woman like Jessie could fall for? Solid, family-oriented, who enjoyed the simple things? Because no question in his mind, his attraction to her could become more if he allowed it to.

Of course, he wouldn't allow it to. He couldn't. He

already had a steep learning curve to climb just building a relationship with his eighteen-month-old son. He sure wasn't fool enough to think he also could master a relationship with the boy's mother.

# Chapter Ten

The aroma of delicious foods competed for customers' attention, and voices careened through the giant room at the decibel of a small jet. Jessie glanced around the crowded community center where the church benefit was being held.

"It looks like half of Noah's Crossing is here," Peter said.

He was right. Not only were half the town's residents there, but many of them were staring at Peter, Jake and Jessie.

Given their unusual circumstances, she could understand people being curious. After all, who wouldn't want to know more about the handsome secret daddy who'd shown up out of the blue?

But she and her family had already given the town enough to talk about. Her accident. Her broken engagement. Clarissa's pregnancy. Clarissa's tragic death. The last thing Jessie wanted was to feed people's curiosity, handsome secret daddy or not. But it might be smart to clue Peter in. "People are staring at us."

"Really." Peter walked beside her with Jake straddling his shoulders. "So what I've heard about small towns is true?"

"Probably."

He gave her a look of amusement. "Let's see. What can we do to feed the gossip mill?"

Her eyes rounded on him. "Don't you dare."

"It might be fun," he teased.

She shot him a quelling look. "Easy for you to say. You don't live here."

"Does gossip really worry you?"

"Not usually," she admitted. So why now? Aiming for normalcy despite the nervous energy pinging inside her ever since Peter strode across that strawberry patch yesterday, Jessie turned her attention to the long table displaying items donated for the silent auction. Everything from football memorabilia to a bread machine to artwork. Her gaze snagged on a familiar, hand-painted vase. "I can't believe Stella Stefano donated her beautiful Victorian vase for the benefit."

"Putty?" Jake pointed from his perch on Peter's shoulders.

"Very pretty," Jessie agreed.

Peter eyed the vase a little suspiciously. "You like antiques?"

"A few special ones. The vase always sat on a shelf in Stella's kitchen, right beside her china clock. I'll miss seeing it there."

Peter's breath stirred her hair as he peered over her shoulder to look at the sheet of paper near the vase. "Only two people have bid on it."

Nerves dancing, she glanced at the paper. "It's worth so much more than those bids."

"How much is it worth?" He brushed her arm as he picked up the pen.

Her nerves had a field day. But the pen in his hand demanded her attention. "What are you doing?"

"I'll bid on it for you."

"Your name on the bidding sheet for an antique vase? I don't think so." She held out her hand for the pen. "I'll bid on it for myself."

He gave her a measured look and handed over the pen.

Jessie considered her bid, then wrote down more than she could afford. "It *is* for a good cause," she rationalized.

"You think that's high enough?" Peter asked.

She squinted at the amount she'd written. "I hope so."

"Hey, Jake." Maggie stopped and gave Jake's leg a tug.

"Maggie." Jake kicked in excitement.

"Take it easy up there, Jake." Chuckling, Peter grasped Jake's churning legs in his long fingers. "Hi, Maggie."

Maggie gave him a cool nod of acknowledgment and turned to Jessie. "I see you bid on the vase. Stella will be thrilled if you get it."

Jessie noted Maggie was being more than a tad snippy to Peter. But what did she expect after she'd told Maggie all her fears about what Peter might do? "I'm surprised she donated it."

"Me, too. She insisted she wanted somebody to have it that would appreciate it. She knows I'm not into antiques. And Tony…well, who knows about Tony? But I need to get a move on. Stella already headed for the car." She waved at Jake.

"Bye." Jake did his imitation of a wave.

Peter bent close to Jessie's ear. "I get the distinct impression Maggie doesn't like me much."

His warm breath gave Jessie goose bumps down her spine. "She's very protective."

"Ah. Then I guess I deserve her disdain, don't I?"

Goose bumps playing tag on her skin, she took a prudent step back. "Yes, you do."

Peter gave her a grimace as if she'd wounded him. "Is Tony her brother?"

Good thing Peter hadn't asked Maggie *that* question. With a last glance at her bid, Jessie began walking through the crowd. "Actually, Tony is Stella's grandson. Stella took Maggie in when her parents died."

"Stella sounds like a generous woman."

Jessie smiled. "She has a huge, Italian heart. And a will to match."

"And Tony?"

"The same. Unfortunately for Maggie, he ditched Noah's Crossing after high school, and he's never been back," Jessie said disgustedly.

"Sounds like Maggie's not the only protective friend."

Jessie nodded. "We've looked out for each other since kindergarten."

"You're both lucky." Peter raised his arm in greeting. "Your mother is waving at us."

"She's selling ice cream and baked goods from the diner."

"Things you baked and donated?"

She nodded.

He gave her a puzzled look. "What time did you start baking this morning to get all that ready?"

"I've been doing extra baking for weeks and storing it in the freezer."

Peter grinned down at her. "Shows you what I know."

He had the most disarming grin. A little lopsided, a tad hesitant as if he didn't often use it. And absolutely bone melting, in her case.

"Think Jake would go for some ice cream?" Peter asked.

She smiled up at Jake. "Want ice cream?"

His face lighting, he clapped his hands and bent for her to take him.

Peter lowered Jake into her arms, his warm gaze holding hers. "How about you? Would you like ice cream?"

The tiny flecks of caramel in his mesmerizing, chocolate eyes made them look even deeper. Richer. More compelling.

"Would a double-chocolate ice cream with butterscotch sprinkles in a wafer cone hit the spot?" Peter asked.

She couldn't help smiling. They'd had ice cream after that first day in the park. "How did you remember all that?"

Peter lifted an eyebrow. "Quick study, remember? And not many people have such definite taste in ice cream."

"I take my food very seriously."

He chuckled.

Had she ever heard a deeper, more masculine chuckle? His chuckle made her smile.

"One double-chocolate with butterscotch sprinkles and wafer cone coming up, Jess."

Mom's voice? Cheeks burning, Jessie tore her gaze from Peter's fascinating eyes to focus on her mother. Lovely. She'd been smiling into Peter's eyes with Mom and half of Noah's Crossing looking on. What was she thinking?

"I'd like a piece of Jessie's blackberry pie," Peter said. "And Jake likes strawberry ice cream in a dish."

No surprise he remembered Jake's preference. But hers? Jessie hid a pleased little smile and resolved to keep her fascination with Peter strictly to herself from here on out.

"Peter can bring food to you and Jake, Jess. Grab Greg's and Mitzi's empty spots." Mom nodded to Jessie's cousin Greg and his very pregnant wife vacating their spots at a long, white, vinyl-draped table crowded with people.

Greg's wife looked so glowing and fulfilled, Jessie's throat closed. Nothing like a reminder of why she had no business being so pleased Peter remembered her favorite ice cream. Nor smiling into his eyes, for that matter.

Jessie moved to claim the vacant chairs. Settling Jake on her lap, she noticed several people stopping to shake hands with Peter as he waited at the counter. For all their curiosity, they were an accepting community of people who cared about one another. And they were welcoming Peter into the fold. He looked so genuinely pleased that she couldn't help being happy for him. She nodded at a woman who served on the worship committee with her.

"One dish of strawberry ice cream for Jake." Peter set the plastic cup in front of Jake. "Please note...I remembered the spoon this time."

"Tunku," Jake took the spoon.

A grin lit Peter's handsome face. "You're very welcome, Jake." He focused his attention on Jessie. "I think I'm beginning to understand him."

The pride and warmth radiating from Peter made Jessie smile as she got Jake started with his ice cream.

Peter handed her cone to her.

"Thanks." She took it from him and caught a drip with her tongue.

He sat down beside her and began eating his pie in earnest.

His closeness kept her so off-balance. She glanced her mom's way.

Her dad had joined her mom behind the counter. And at the moment, both parents were watching and smiling their approval. Apparently, Peter was winning them over, too. Jessie concentrated fiercely on her ice-cream cone.

"The woman who's in charge of the auction introduced herself," Peter said. "I asked her to watch that vase. If anybody bids over you, she promised to put in a higher bid."

"Oh, no," Jessie moaned.

He gave her a puzzled look. "I thought the vase meant a lot to you."

"It does. Thank you." She didn't have the heart to tell him how much people would love talking about the thoughtful thing Peter was doing for her. Nor how quickly the news would spread and pique people's fruitful imaginations. Everybody would have them locked in their minds as a couple for sure. As a ready-made family, for that matter.

She bit her lip. But before people did any such matching up, they'd have to finish discussing the fact that Peter first had been Clarissa's. Lovely. But if Peter hadn't been with Clarissa, she wouldn't have Jake, now would she?

"Hi, Jessie," a child's voice greeted.

Jessie turned. "How are you doing, Amy?"

"Good." The first grader smiled at Jake, exposing a gap in her teeth that hadn't been there last week. "Hi, Jake."

"Amy," Jake squealed, pointing to his bowl. "Cweam. Ummm."

The little girl's dimples flashed. "Strawberry? It looks good, Jake."

"Amy is my cousin Bill's daughter," Jessie explained. "Amy, this is Peter."

"Hi." Amy shyly ducked her head.

"Nice to meet you, Amy. I'm Jake's daddy."

Amy's blond head popped up. "Jake's daddy?"

"Sure thing." Peter grinned.

"No." Jake pointed to Peter. "Pedo."

Jessie's heart contracted. He didn't understand how significant his correction was. "Peter is your daddy, sweetheart."

Jake shook his head and pointed at Peter again. "Pedo."

She met Peter's eyes. "He doesn't understand."

"I know. But thank you for telling him," Peter said softly.

"Are you and Jessie married?" Amy asked.

"No," Peter answered.

Amy frowned up at Jessie. "If you're not married, how can he be Jake's daddy?"

Peter raised an eyebrow at Jessie.

Did he think *she'd* know how to explain their situation to a six-year-old?

"Amy, would you like ice cream?" Peter asked.

Amy smiled, the gap in her front teeth prominently displayed. "Strawberry with a regular cone, please."

Winking at Jessie, he stood, grasped Amy's hand and strolled to the counter with her, her blond curls bouncing.

Her mom listened attentively to Peter's request, an approving smile lifting her lips.

No question, Peter would be a wonderful dad to the bunch of kids he wanted someday. As happy as Jessie was for him, she couldn't help feeling sad for herself. She concentrated on her ice cream.

Peter strode back alone.

Glancing around for Amy, Jessie spotted her talking up a storm with her mom. "You're a natural with children."

He gave her a devastating smile she'd never seen before. "That's a major compliment, coming from you."

All she could do was return his smile and try to remember how to breathe as understanding seeped into her addled mind. People gossiping about Peter being Clarissa's guy, or him and Jessie being a couple or the three of them being a ready-made family wasn't what really bothered her, was it? What bothered her was that being a couple/family was what *she* was starting to want.

And what she could never have.

"Jess?" her mom said softly.

Jessie opened her eyes. She'd rocked Jake long after she'd felt his body relax against her in sleep. Now, the light in the hallway outlined her mom's slim figure. Jessie stood and laid her sweet boy in his crib. She drew his blanket over his sturdy little body, turned and followed her mother down the hall.

"I made tea. Want to have a tea chat?"

"Okay." She was sure her mom was as aware as she was that the last "tea chat" they'd had included Clarissa right before she'd gone back to New York. Two weeks later, she'd died trying to save her research in a lab fire. Apparently, Mom thought it was time to reclaim the tradition they'd had since she and Clarissa were very young.

Maybe a conversation with her mom would take Jessie's mind off Peter. His nightly calls were quickly becoming part of Jake's bedtime ritual. And knowing she shouldn't look forward to hearing his deep voice on the other end of the line as much as Jake did didn't seem to stop her. She pulled out a chair at the table and slumped into it.

Her mom sat opposite her, beginning the familiar ritual by pouring tea from the china teapot that had belonged to Jessie's great-great-grandmother. She handed Jessie a cup.

"Thanks." Drawing in the scent of spiced tea, Jessie took a careful sip. "I miss Rissa so much."

"I know, dear. So do I. But I'd expect you'd be on top of the world with the way things are working out with Peter and Jake."

Jessie nodded. "I'm very happy about that, Mom."

Her mother gave a slight shake of her head. "You don't act happy."

"I *am*. I'm *very* happy," she insisted. She certainly wasn't going to talk about Peter's thoughtfulness during his calls. Or that he always asked about her day, shared events of his own day and encouraged her comments as if he cared what she thought.

Mom's gaze ran over her as if looking for someplace that hurt. "Are you well?"

"I'm fine."

"No, Jessie, you aren't fine."

Jessie took another sip of tea, set it on the table and faked a yawn. "Nothing a good night's sleep won't fix."

Her mom shook her head. "Save that hogwash for somebody who doesn't know you."

"Hogwash? I've never heard you use that word before." Jessie forced a laugh. "You worry too much, Mom."

"Worrying is part of my job description. So is knowing when something is wrong with my daughter. And I'm very good at both."

"Well, this time, your barometer is off."

"So how is Peter?"

"Peter?" Jessie gave her mother a serious frown. How did Peter get into this conversation again?

"You talk to him on the phone every night. You must know how he is."

He was lonely. Jessie heard it in his voice, in his silences. And she felt responsible for it. Because if he hadn't left Jake with her, he wouldn't be lonely, would he? "Peter's great. He's very encouraged because his friend with ALS seems to be responding to the experimental drug Peter developed."

"That's wonderful." Her mom sighed. "I know you too well, Jess, not to sense your excitement when he calls. I haven't heard you sound like that since Neil."

"Mother." Jessie closed her eyes and let out a shaky breath. "There's nothing between Peter and me but Jake."

Her dad walked into the kitchen.

Jessie held her breath, hoping he hadn't overheard.

She never stood a chance when her parents ganged up on her.

He met her eyes. "Nothing between you and Peter except Jake?"

Jessie let out her breath.

"Your mother and I are getting older, Jess, but we can't miss the obvious. Peter looks at you like you're the best thing since plum pudding. I haven't forgotten looking at your mother that way." He looked at her mother now, a twinkle in his eye.

Her mom's eyes crinkled in a satisfied little smile.

"Not everybody is as lucky as you two, Dad. And you don't have to worry about Peter. I've told you before—I don't want a man in my life." It was time to end this chat. "I'm going to turn in. I'm beat." She started to get up.

"Not so fast," her dad said in his voice of authority.

She sat back down. You'd think she was still twelve.

"When you and Neil broke off your engagement, you wouldn't talk to us about it, so your mother and I backed off to give you time to heal."

"I know how disappointed you were."

"Good heavens." Her mother sounded surprised. "We liked Neil, of course. But you've never disappointed us, Jess. We were sorry for your loss is all. And sorry it happened while you were still recovering from the accident."

"Thank God Jake brought you back to us," her dad said. "But you can't tell me you're not turning down every interested man who asks you out. And it's not healthy. It's time to move on, put the past completely behind you."

"I've done that, Dad." She had, hadn't she?

He shook his head. "You obviously haven't."

Her mom set her cup on the table. "Maybe we could help you more if you'd tell us what's wrong."

"I'm doing just fine, Mom. And you both help more than you know."

Dad patted her hand. "When you were little, we used to watch you put every last one of your dolls to bed before you went to sleep. And you're a wonderful mother to Jake. We know how important having a family is to you, sweetheart."

"Yes," she whispered, unable to trust her voice.

"Well, how do you plan to have the family you've always wanted if you don't put Neil behind you and find somebody else?"

She had trouble breathing. Her dad didn't know he'd plunged a knife into her heart.

He cleared his throat. "Peter's a good man. It couldn't have been an easy decision for him to put his son's needs first. But I couldn't respect him more for making it."

She narrowed her eyes, fearing where her dad was headed. "I know."

"I'm feeling much better about Peter than I did at first, too, dear." Her mom smiled.

"Are you both forgetting he and *Clarissa* had a baby together?"

"Of course not. And I know that might be hard for you to get past. But Dad's right. Peter is proving himself to be an honorable man, and God sent him here for a reason. Wouldn't it be wonderful if you and Peter ended up giving Jake a united family?"

"What?" She couldn't believe her ears. Wasn't fighting her feelings for Peter hard enough? The last thing she needed was a cheering section. One more thing to drive herself crazy about. She pushed herself up from the table. "It's never going to happen, Mom."

Turning, she marched out of the room before either of her parents could stop her.

# Chapter Eleven

**P**eter stood in the crowded shop admiring the shiny black bike he'd just purchased. Aluminum frame and rims, trigger shift, linear pull brakes. Who knew if he needed all that, but he figured buying quality usually worked out in the end. Anyway, it was a great-looking bike, it fit him and the store would install a child's seat on the back while he waited. "I need a similar woman's bike, too." Buying a bike for Jessie was even more exciting than buying one for himself. "She's about five-six. I'm not sure about her torso length, though."

"Can she come in to have the bike fitted?" the salesman asked.

"Afraid not. She lives out of town, and I want to take the bike with me." It would be a lot of fun riding together this weekend on that great bike trail that ran around Rainbow Lake.

"A medium torso length should work. The info you learned when we fit yours should help you figure out if the bike fits her properly. And when she's in town, have her bring it in and we can make adjustments."

"Great."

"Color preference?"

Jessie's clear blue eyes came to mind. She often wore blue, too. Scanning the bikes taking up most of the room, Peter smiled and pointed to just the thing. "How about that pretty blue one over there?"

"Perfect."

"And I need those helmets we talked about." Peter took the paper from his pocket with head sizes jotted on it. Jessie's mother had been more than happy to help him out when he'd called earlier. He handed the paper to the salesman.

The salesman nodded. "I'm sure I have these sizes in stock. We'll have you set in no time." Turning on his heel, he grasped the handlebars of Peter's new bike. "We'll install that child's seat. And just so you know, we always deflate the tires a little to make a softer ride for the kid. They sit right over the axle and feel the bumps more than the adult rider will. We want biking to be a great experience for everybody."

"Thanks."

"No problem." He wheeled the bike into the back room.

Peter couldn't help grinning. He hoped Jessie and Jake got half the pleasure out of biking as he did buying the bikes for them. He couldn't wait to show them.

He sighed a satisfied sigh. He didn't know what happened between Jessie and Neil to bring them to break their engagement, but why should it affect Peter's relationship with her? After all, Neil was part of her past, wasn't he? He had nothing to do with the here and now.

Peter was here and now. And he'd meant every word he'd said in his email to her. He wanted to win her trust and earn the privilege of being Jake's dad. After the terrific time they'd had together last weekend, he was beginning to think he was well on his way.

Because no getting around it...he liked her. He liked who he was when he was with her. Talking to her on the phone at Jake's bedtime was the best part of his day. So why wouldn't he want to be with her as much as he possibly could?

After closing the diner, Jessie pulled on her paint-spattered jeans and old pink T-shirt and threw open the windows in her little apartment over the diner. Breathing in the scent of fresh paint, she turned up the volume on her CD player and set to work painting her bedroom walls dusky periwinkle. She'd taken the color from the floral pattern in a vintage tablecloth she'd found at a flea market and planned to use to sew curtains for the two small windows in the room.

Her little sanctuary was beginning to come together. If all went well, she'd finish the bedroom tonight. The rest would have to wait until next week because Peter would be in town this weekend.

She bit her lip and forbade the anticipation that set her nerves on edge. He'd had to cancel at the last minute last weekend. Some problem came up at work. But he planned to be here tomorrow night. She'd organized Jake's scrapbooks to show him.

And things seemed to be going well. All she had to do was keep things the way they were and maintain a level head about her son's good-looking daddy and everything would be fine. Listening to her music, Jessie finished painting one wall and began the second, pausing to swipe tears from her eyes at the last strains of "Over the Rainbow."

A noise behind her made her whirl around. She almost jumped out of her skin.

Peter filled the doorway, tall and powerful, his handsome face glowing with emotion.

Undoubtedly emotion brought on by her CD. Her heart sang just seeing him again. She smiled in spite of the sudden lack of air in the room. "This music is so pure, I always respond to it, too."

He searched her eyes as if he didn't understand her comment.

"The music," she explained.

Holding her gaze, he took a step closer. "Jessie...it's not the music...."

"No?"

He shook his head.

She felt tension stretching between them like a rubber band about to snap. Still, she couldn't look away.

Blowing out a breath, he turned, ducked to avoid bumping his head on the sloped ceiling, then walked over and picked up the CD cover.

She attempted to get her bearings. What just happened? She wasn't sure. All she knew was it was something powerful. Something that, if left unchecked, would blow the status quo right out of the water.

"Did you know your downstairs door is unlocked?" he asked huskily.

"Yes."

"You should lock it when you're working alone at night."

Was he concerned about her? "We have no crime rate in Noah's Crossing, Peter."

"No point in inviting one." He laid the CD cover down, his gaze scanning the room. "So this is your work in progress?"

Good. He was aiming for light. Even if her bedroom did feel too small. "It's Thursday. I mean… What are you doing here?"

He rubbed the back of his neck. "It's been almost two weeks—a very long two weeks."

She saw the strain and exhaustion in his face. A twinge of guilt reminded her that he worked super-human hours all week, then had to drive four hours to see his son because she didn't want to move to Madison. Another factor in maintaining the status quo? "Jake's been asking about you."

He grinned his crooked grin. "Yeah?"

Her heart melted at his wistful tone. "Several times a day."

His grin broadened.

He had the most captivating smile, one mostly re-served for Jake, even the mention of him. She couldn't help smiling back.

"I've missed him." He held her gaze for a long moment. "And I've missed you, Jessie."

"I've missed you, too." The words were out before she could stop them.

"Yeah?" He smiled.

She squinted, willing him not to pursue her comment further.

"I brought a couple surprises with me."

Letting out a grateful breath, she raised an eyebrow. "A *couple* surprises?"

"You'll have to come down to my car to see one of them." He motioned to the half-painted wall. "But go ahead, finish painting that wall before it dries."

She hesitated. What would he do while she painted? Watch her? "I'll finish it later."

"You sure?"

She nodded, capped the paint can, tucked the roller in a plastic bag to keep it moist and tied it with a twist tie.

"Slick trick," he commented. "Does it work?"

"Like a dream." She felt like she was in a dream. And she needed to snap out of it.

"How about giving me a tour of your place first?"

She studied him a moment to determine if he was kidding.

"Please?" He sounded sincere enough.

She loved showing off her little place to whoever was interested. "Well…this room will be my bedroom."

"Pretty blue."

"Periwinkle." She self-consciously walked past him into the hall.

"Tell me what you've done," he urged.

"I stripped layers and layers of wallpaper off the walls and primed and painted everything."

He looked up. "Ceilings, too?"

"Absolutely." Pushing open the door, she led Peter into Jake's room with its cloud ceiling, woodland murals and imaginary creatures flying and scampering everywhere.

Peter's glance swept the room, his lips quirking in a smile. "This is fantastic."

"I did *his* room first. It was so much fun."

"He must love playing here."

"I've shown it to him, but I don't let him play here with all the dust and paint fumes in the air."

Peter shook his head. "I wouldn't have thought of that."

"You'll develop kind of a sixth sense about him, too."

"You think I will?" he asked eagerly.

"Of course." She gave him a smile of encouragement. Her heart seemed to swell every time he said or did something that so clearly demonstrated his love for Jake. Before she could get all syrupy, she led the way to her favorite room—the kitchen. "The room's just big enough to hold a future table in front of the double windows. The vase you bought at the auction will be the perfect centerpiece."

"I'm glad you got it."

"Aunt Lou said you gave her the money, and I want to pay you for it."

"Absolutely not. The money was my donation to the fundraiser." His tone was final. "And the vase is a gift."

A gift sounded personal. She shook her head.

"Not accepting my gift would be rude. Besides, if you don't accept it, what will I do with a fancy antique vase with flowers painted all over it?"

Jessie reconsidered. "Well…if you put it that way… thank you."

"You're very welcome." Peter ran his hand over the detailed mosaic backsplash. "You didn't do this, did you?"

"I did. It was fun, but it took more time than I expected."

"It's beautiful, Jessie."

"Thank you." He really did seem impressed.

"You're a woman of many talents."

His praise felt so good. She was pleased the complicated pattern she'd designed turned out well. And she was even more pleased Peter appreciated the things she'd done.

In the postage-stamp-size bathroom he admired the original pedestal sink and black-and-white tile floor.

And in the living room, the colorful, lead glass panel topping the windows garnered his praise.

"That's it," she said proudly.

He looked genuinely impressed. "The place has a lot of character. You're working miracles with it."

"Thank you." She hadn't felt so strong and capable for a very long time.

He grinned. "Thanks for the tour. I look forward to seeing the place finished."

"It will be a while. Sanding and refinishing the floors will be a big project."

"I'd be glad to help out on weekends after we put Jake to bed."

Jessie bit her lip. "Thanks, but I can't ask you to do that."

"Why not? I'm sure I wouldn't meet your high standards. I've never done this kind of work. But if you want heavy lifting or something that doesn't take any finesse, I'm your man."

A vision popped into her mind of him lifting a heavy piece of furniture, muscles bulging. She swallowed against a bevy of butterflies fluttering in her stomach.

"You want to go to my car to see the surprise now?"

She nodded, grateful for a change of venue. Fresh air and wide-open spaces would do her good. She watched him duck low to avoid the scaffolding over the steps, then followed him down the stairs and outside to his SUV parked at the curb.

He strode to the rear of the vehicle, pulled open the tailgate doors and reached inside. He lifted out a shiny, black bike complete with child's seat on the back and looked at her, excitement in his eyes. "Don't worry. I bought helmets. Jake loves to go fast on swings and slides, so I figure he'll love bike riding."

She smiled at his enthusiasm. "I'm sure he'll love it."

"Will you have time tomorrow to go for a ride?"

"I don't have a bike."

"Good. Then I won't have to return this." He reached in the back of his vehicle and dragged out a blue women's bike. "It's not exactly periwinkle, but you often wear blue so I figure you must like it."

He'd even thought about her favorite color. But what was he thinking? Expensive gifts definitely crossed the line. "It's beautiful, but it's too expensive, Peter. I can't—"

He raised his hand to stop her. "Please don't put a price tag on my surprise. All I want to know is if it's a hit."

She frowned and tried to figure out how best to handle this.

"Consider it a gift to Jake and me. We want you to go with us."

"I suppose…if you put it that way…" She gave him a hesitant thumbs-up.

"Great." He lifted the bikes back into the SUV, slammed the doors and strode to the passenger door where he took out a large, leather case. "Let's go inside. We need light for you to see these."

"What is it?"

"I took your advice and hired a decorator. This case contains a few computer-generated preliminary sketches I picked up on my way out of town. I'm anxious to see them."

"You don't waste time," she said in surprise.

"Sleeping on the floor in the middle of nothing will do that to a guy." He strode to the side door that led to her apartment.

She hurried to keep up.

He pulled open the door and waited for her to lead the way up the stairs. Ducking under the scaffolding, she reached the upstairs hall and strode into the cleanly swept living room. She sat down on the old pine floor. "We can spread out the drawings here."

He lowered himself beside her, opened the case and removed the drawings.

Sitting so close she could feel his warmth probably wasn't the best idea. Reluctantly, she scooched over.

He smoothed out a drawing in front of them. "A basic sketch of the great room with the open kitchen on the end."

She peered at the rich woods, soaring beamed ceiling and floor-to-ceiling windows and drew in a breath of admiration. "This is gorgeous, Peter."

"I like the architecture. But the condo is empty and cold."

"The woods make it warmer than I envisioned when you talked about it." Ideas began flashing through her mind of more ways to warm it up. "A warm color paint will help, and you can use furniture placement to divide it into cozy living areas."

"I like the sound of that." He spread another sketch over the first one. "This seems to be what the decorator came up with for that area."

Jessie peered at the heavy draperies, pretentious furnishings and overdone architectural enhancements. "This doesn't look anything like you, Peter." She looked up at him. "Did you tell the decorator what you had in mind?"

"I tried."

"And this is what she—"

"He."

"He sketched for you?"

Peter frowned at the drawing. "Am I missing something? Or is it sanctimonious, oppressive and pretentious?"

"Exactly," she agreed.

Unfortunately, the drawings for Jake's room were just as bad.

"You need a different decorator, Peter. One that's more in tune with the kind of home you want."

"Or maybe I need help explaining what I want."

She frowned up at him. "I've never known you to be at a loss for words."

"I think using the *right* words is my problem."

"I can't imagine how a decorator could more thoroughly misunderstand that you want a warm, comfortable, child-friendly home."

"I'm glad I ran this by you. I would be miserable living in this place if I'd accepted his interpretation."

"You wouldn't have accepted this, would you?"

He shrugged. "I've ignored some pretty bad surroundings in the furnished apartments I've rented."

"You've never owned your own place?"

He shook his head. "I'm never home except to sleep. But I want a home now. And I hope you'll bring Jake to Madison to visit. As often as possible."

She bit her lip. Madison was the last place she wanted to go. But Peter was driving so far to see Jake. How could she let him do all the compromising where Jake was concerned? She focused on the decorator's ideas again. Pitiful.

"Can you give me a few suggestions to convey to a decorator?"

"I can't just look at a drawing and come up with anything specific, Peter. I have to feel the space."

"Well, in that case, how soon will a trip to Madison work for you?"

She looked at him blankly, then realized what she'd said. Obviously, a trip to Madison *was* what it would take for her to feel the space, wasn't it? Dragging a breath, she shot Peter a doubtful look.

"Remember, I'm camping out on the floor in the middle of nothing. My one convenience is a package of disposable glasses so I can take a drink of water without slurping it from the faucet. Help me. Please?" He looked at her pleadingly.

She rolled her eyes at his "poor me" expression. "And this is my problem, why?"

He raised a dark eyebrow. "Because you are a compassionate human being."

"That's the best you can come up with?"

Giving her a half-grin, he tapped his index finger on the stack of drawings. "You're not going to throw *Jake's dad* to the decorating wolves, are you?"

She harrumphed.

"Tell you what…I'll rent a car and leave the SUV for you to drive down. It has a DVD player in the back to occupy Jake on the trip."

A nightmare of crashing metal bombarded her memory. Smells of spilled gas and oil. Chilling screams. Searing pain. "It's impossible."

"But I'm desperate. Sleeping-on-the-floor desperate."

She shook her head. She couldn't drive on the freeway. No way would she be comfortable driving in all that traffic. "I'd have to find help to cover the diner.

I'm not sure how Jake would handle four hours in the car."

Shaking his head, Peter rubbed the back of his neck as if he wasn't buying her excuses.

And why should he? Hadn't he accepted her terms on just about everything with Jake? Would it kill her to do something for him for a change? "When I close the diner Sunday afternoon, maybe Jake and I can ride down with you then. Oh wait, that won't work. How would we get home?"

He brightened. "Drive the SUV back to Noah's Crossing. I'll rent a car for the week."

Same problem. She'd have to drive on the freeway. "Or we could take the bus home." She pressed her fingers to her forehead. "This is getting awfully complicated."

"Not at all."

She realized she hadn't even considered another complication. "Even if the DVD player helps Jake on the trip down, I can't make him sit in his seat all the way home again."

"You and Jake will stay with me, of course."

She frowned.

"I have four bedrooms, Jessie. The master bedroom is downstairs, so you and Jake will have the entire second floor to yourselves. I'm having a king mattress and spring delivered tomorrow. I'll call the store and have them deliver two sets and tell them to throw in a crib."

"I have a Pack 'N Play for Jake. And we'll stay in a motel."

He raised an eyebrow. "You'll be safer at my place."

She wasn't so sure, given the butterflies playing havoc in her stomach. She gave him a serious frown.

"Okay. You win. I'll make a reservation. And everything will work out fine. You'll see."

Easy for him to say.

# Chapter Twelve

The drone of heavy interstate traffic assaulted her. Jessie dragged her gaze from the speedometer and focused on Peter's strong hands on the steering wheel. His long, capable fingers expertly guided the SUV in and out of traffic that had gotten much heavier in the past five minutes. She'd never seen so many cars and semis and recreational vehicles flying down the highway. Nobody realized how quickly one distracted driver could change all these people's lives forever.

She blew her hair off her forehead. How had she let Peter talk her into making this trip? She wasn't ready. Wanting to be ready didn't mean she could do it. *Please keep us safe, God. And please don't let me throw up.*

"To make a long story short," Peter continued his tale about a boarding-school experience. "The students regretted stealing the questions from my dorm room when they all flunked their tests the next morning."

"You told the teacher?"

Peter shook his head. "He would have expelled them. I didn't want that on my conscience, so I worked half the night on another group of questions."

Tamping down her tension, she tried to smile. "Good save."

"It worked. They never tried that prank again."

She liked him sharing things about his life with her. Obviously, his teachers recognized he was a very gifted student and gave him a lot of responsibility. But she heard the undertow of loneliness in the humorous stories he'd been sharing about growing up in boarding schools. Deep loneliness that made her want to put her arms around him and make it all go away.

How ridiculous was that? She couldn't even make her own fears go away. She eyed vehicles bumper to bumper, vying for position at breakneck speeds and gripped the seat a little tighter. Why was everybody in such a hurry?

"Hungry?" Peter asked.

"What?"

"It's almost six. I don't have food at my place, so we need to stop at a restaurant for dinner."

The thought of food was not a good one right now. Besides, Jake had been an angel the entire trip, either napping or captivated by Thomas DVDs. But all his inactivity would cost them once his feet hit the ground. "Jake will need to run off steam. I don't think we want to turn him loose in a restaurant."

"Well, there's a little pizza place around the corner from my condo that's run by an Italian family. Can Jake eat pizza?"

"If it's not too spicy. But I brought food for him in the cooler in the back."

"Great. The place is near your motel. We'll drop off your things and pick up a pizza. They make the best I've ever tasted. I've been keeping them in business ever since I moved."

"Not much of a cook?"

"To try cooking, I'd need to go to a grocery store. And I wouldn't have a clue what to buy."

She cringed as a semi roared past at the speed of light.

Peter glanced at her. "The traffic bothers you, doesn't it?"

She dragged a breath, her uneasy stomach rolling. "I hate the interstate," she said through tight lips.

"Your accident happened on the interstate?"

She nodded. "Not far ahead."

"I'm sorry, Jessie. I could have taken other roads."

"The interstate's faster." She hoped the wobble in her voice didn't give her away. "I'm fine."

He nodded, apparently accepting her at her word. "We're getting close to the Wisconsin Dells tourist area. Besides that, a lot of people are going home after spending the weekend away. It won't be this bad tomorrow when you drive back. Of course, you can take back roads if you'd be more comfortable."

"I think the bus is a better option." Suddenly, the car to their left shot into their lane. "Peter!"

He braked, expertly allowing the errant car to merge. "Take a few deep breaths, Jessie. You're white as a sheet."

Gripping her forehead, she shut her eyes and tried to calm down.

"It was bad, wasn't it?" he asked, concern in his voice.

She swallowed, not wanting to remember, but memories came anyway. "I was pinned in the car. By the time they got me out, I was in a pretty bad way. They med-flighted me to U.W. Hospital."

He blew out a breath. "You were driving?"

"No." She kept her eyes closed, trying not to relive the nightmare that now woke her only occasionally. "Neil was driving."

"Was he hurt, too?"

"Scrapes and bruises."

"Was he at fault?"

"He was shuffling through CDs, and he blamed himself for not braking soon enough. But even if he could have stopped in time, the car behind us would have still slammed into us."

"How long were you in the hospital?"

"Three months, and two more in the rehab center. I completed physical therapy in Eau Claire, which made it a little easier for my parents." She heard her voice go on and on as if she were talking about somebody else.

"You did a great job in rehab."

Rehab couldn't solve everything though. She opened her eyes. "At first, doctors predicted I'd be in a wheelchair. But God took good care of me."

His brow furrowed.

She knew he didn't believe in prayer. She could understand that. There'd been times when she'd had trouble, as well. But his expression said something was bothering him. "What is it?"

"I don't understand how you think God took good care of you. After all you've been through."

"Because He did. In the accident, in several surgeries… But believe me, I was angry and buried in self-pity for a good long while."

"How did you get past it?"

"On one impossible day in therapy, praying was the only way I could get through the pain." Her stomach ached just thinking of that day. "I'd never in my life felt so defeated and alone and hopeless. All I was able to do was say God's name, and somehow, He was there. Comforting. Easing the pain. Making me stronger." She took a deep breath. "I was raised in the church, but prayer didn't become real to me until that day."

"I've been doing some reading about prayer since we talked about it."

"Really?" She was a little surprised.

"Do you feel praying changed you that day?"

"Changed me?"

"Something I read about praying being not so much asking for what you want as asking to be changed in ways you can't imagine."

She turned his words over in her mind. "Yes. That was how I felt." She hadn't had those words before to describe the way God touched her that day, but they fit perfectly.

Slowing, Peter took an exit ramp off the interstate.

"Do we need gas again?"

"No. Interstate traffic will be even heavier the rest of the way to Madison. I think you'll be more comfortable driving at a slower pace."

He was taking care of her, and surprisingly, she didn't resent it. Instead, warmth unfurled inside her like a blossom in spring. She laid her hand on his arm. "Thank you, Peter."

Spicy smells of pizza still in the air, Jake's squeals bounced off the hard surfaces of Peter's soaring kitchen like a pickup game in a gymnasium. On his hands and knees, the little guy scrambled around the corner of the island pushing a giant truck.

Peter thundered after him also on his hands and knees pushing a truck. He almost ran square into Jessie's legs. "Whoops."

"Watch it." She set their empty soda cans on the counter, the pizza box still in her hand.

He grinned up at her as if crawling around on the floor was a normal thing for a grown man to do. "Are you aware you're entering a construction zone?"

Her warm smile eclipsed the sadness in her eyes. "Not as aware as your neighbors are, I'm sure."

He laughed. "They'll be shocked sounds are coming from my place." He loved that she'd opened up to him on the way down about her accident. Loved that she'd risked coming to Madison in the first place. Maybe he was winning her trust?

Probably a good thing he hadn't kissed her that night at her apartment when he'd walked in to find her painting and crying to her music. He'd been thinking about kissing her ever since. But trust needed to come first. He sure didn't want to do anything to send her hiding from him again. "You're my guest. You shouldn't be cleaning up after us."

"There's not much to clean up. Besides, I'm getting stiff just sitting. I need to walk around a bit."

"Pedo," Jake hollered.

"Be right there, pal. I'm talking to your mommy."

"Do you have a container to save the leftover pizza?" Jessie asked.

"Just set the box in the fridge. I'll eat the pizza for breakfast."

"You are joking, I hope."

"Uh-oh. I forgot you take your food seriously."

Rolling her eyes, she walked over and pulled open his oversize, stainless-steel refrigerator. "There's plenty of room. Jake's food and snacks from the cooler are the only things in here."

"Pedo," Jake yelled again. "Brocks." On his knees, he held up a block in each hand for Peter to see.

"I think my buddy's getting impatient." Tearing himself away from Jessie, Peter thundered over to his son and set about helping him build a block tower.

Jessie circled the room, apparently getting some exercise. "Are you planning to buy pans and dishes? Or will you leave all those beautiful cupboards of yours empty?"

Aware of her whereabouts at any given moment, Peter guided Jake's little hand to place a block on top of the stack. "That depends. Will you help me fill them?"

"I could help you buy dishes and pots and pans and spices—but unless you plan to cook, I guess there's not much point in filling your cupboards, is there?"

"Sure there is. If you tell me what to buy, I'll have whatever you need when you and Jake are here."

"I have a diner to run, remember? Don't fill the cupboards just for Jake and me."

Who else was he going to fill them for? But she'd made her point. Just because she'd agreed to come to Madison this time didn't mean he could take future trips for granted.

They couldn't come often enough for him. Funny, his place didn't have a stick of furniture, but it didn't feel empty anymore. Not with Jake and Jessie filling it with more love than he knew how to deal with.

"But you need a coffeemaker to brew yourself a cup of coffee in the morning. And a toaster to make a piece of toast. And butter. Maybe honey and jam?"

He liked her fussing over what he ate. He liked it a lot. "Sounds great. I could buy bread and coffee at convenience stores when I get gas."

"Bang!" Jake swung his arm and the block tower crashed loudly to the floor.

Peter laughed. "Good job, big guy. Shall we build another tower?"

Not answering, Jake crawled away and began zooming a small car along the floor.

Jessie sat down on the hearth of the towering stone fireplace.

"I think I'll give my knees a rest on this trip, Jake." Peter climbed to his feet, walked over and sat on the hearth beside Jessie, her familiar lemon scent drawing him in.

"I brought a few magazines for you to go through tonight and rip out pictures that strike you. It will help you get a feel for things you like before we go shopping tomorrow. And you can share the pictures with your decorator," she said.

He raised an eyebrow. "You're giving me homework?"

"Yep. I'm giving myself homework, too. If you let me take your Sunday paper to the motel with me, I'll study ads and figure out where we can look at furniture tomorrow."

"Sounds good. By the way, Scott and Karen invited us to stop over before you leave. They want to meet you and Jake."

"I'd love to meet them."

He couldn't wait to show Jake and Jessie off. He smiled at Jake talking away to his car in a language all his own. "I've been meaning to tell you, I took out a life-insurance policy that will continue to grow for him."

"That's thoughtful, Peter. Clarissa left a trust for him, too."

"Good for her. Jessie, I don't resent her anymore for not telling me about Jake. She knew you'd be the best mother for him. She had no idea I'd want to be a father. Actually, neither did I until I met the little guy. She obviously did what she thought was best for the baby during a very stressful time."

Jessie smiled. "She cared more than anybody thinks. She was a wonderful sister. I still miss her every day."

Her words moving him, he grasped her hand, her skin warm and smooth to his touch.

She held on.

"Jessie, will you let me take care of him financially?"

She squinted at him.

"He's my son. I need to do this."

She gave a nod.

"Yeah?" He grinned, pleasantly surprised she'd agreed. And without an argument to boot. "Thank you."

She met his eyes. "Have you looked into changing his birth certificate to include your name?"

Surprised by her question, he searched her face. "Would you be all right with that?"

"Your name should be on his birth certificate, Peter."

"You know how much it would mean to me?"

"Yes."

Of course she knew. "Jessie, I'd put your name on his birth certificate, too, if I could."

Tears sparkled in her eyes. "Thank you," she whispered.

Never taking his gaze from hers, he reached out and laid his free hand along her jaw.

Her eyes widened invitingly.

He smiled, even if he had forgotten how to breathe. Kissing her the only thing on his mind, he moved closer.

She pulled back just enough to discourage him.

Smile dying, he took his hand from her face. "I like you, Jessie."

"I like you, too." She swallowed. "As a friend."

"What about more than friends?"

She took her hand from his. "We need to think of Jake."

"Always." But she wasn't making sense. "I don't see how more than friendship between us could possibly be a bad thing for him, though, do you?"

She frowned. "You have to be kidding."

"Why do you say that?"

"Given our situation? Peter, we could never walk away from each other when things didn't work out."

"That's pretty pessimistic, don't you think? Who says things won't work out?"

"Experience."

"You're referring to your broken engagement?"

She gave a nod.

"Can you tell me what happened?"

She shook her head and pointed to Jake lying on the floor singing to his car. "He's going to fall asleep. We need to take him to the motel."

"In a minute. Jessie, if I don't know what happened with your engagement, how can I understand why you think things can't work out between us?"

She sighed. Staring at the floor, she folded her arms across her chest in defensive mode. "We were engaged our junior year in college, and we'd just started senior year when the accident happened. The next few months are a blur. I was in the hospital and in physical therapy, but he drove to Madison to see me almost every weekend." She pressed her hand to her forehead.

He hated putting her through this, but how could he help her move past it if he didn't know what happened? He stroked her arm. "Please go on."

She blew out a breath. "I've never told anyone what happened."

"Maybe it will help if you do."

She peered into his eyes as if looking for something. Reassurance? Compassion? Understanding? "One day he was driving me home to stay with my parents for a while, and he told me he was transferring to UCLA. He said he couldn't marry me. That he couldn't deal with his guilt after the accident." She put her hand to her throat.

A weight seemed to descend to Peter's chest. She didn't have to tell him how devastated she'd been. He could see it in her eyes. "I'm sorry, Jessie."

He wanted to blame Neil for not being strong enough to handle his guilt over the accident. After all, Jessie forgave the guy. What more did he need? But Neil hadn't been a winner in this, either. He'd lost Jessie. "One thing you need to know—I will never hurt you like that. Never."

Sighing, she studied him as if mulling over his words. "I almost believe you." She lifted her chin as if she'd made a decision. "But the stakes with Jake are too high, Peter. I won't take a chance."

Her words hit him hard, her tone so final. Together, they seemed to leave no room for compromise. He looked away. "I'm sorry you feel that way."

He couldn't deny it. He was hurt. He was disappointed. And he'd never felt more alone.

# Chapter Thirteen

"You must like green or you wouldn't have bought the shirt you're wearing." Jessie's voice sounded almost as raw as her nerves. Surrounded by furniture displays and the smells of new everything, she felt completely overwhelmed by the huge selection the store carried. Whatever possessed her to think she could remember enough from her college courses in decorating to advise Peter on furniture for his new condo?

Subdued and withdrawn ever since he'd picked her and Jake up at the motel, he looked down at his polo shirt as if noticing its color for the first time. "I bought it because it's comfortable."

She gave her head a little shake. "Do you like green?"

He bent and adjusted the stroller to support sleeping Jake's head. "It's okay."

How noncommittal could he get? "I can see you feel passionately about color."

Straightening, he gave her a raised eyebrow without any hint of amusement.

She sighed. Clearly, he hadn't forgotten her rejection last night any more than she had. She hadn't forgotten his touch, either. Nor the admiration in his eyes. She'd wanted him to kiss her so much.

Before she'd come to her senses.

And she understood completely why he was withdrawn and quiet. Rejection was never easy. She'd hurt him. She felt terrible about that, but she'd had to end any speculation he might have about a relationship that could never happen. Not telling him the whole truth about why also weighed heavily on her conscience.

She sighed. If only she could get her mind off last night and on to furniture shopping. As it was, she was floundering in a big way. "I don't know what made me think I could help you with your condo, Peter."

He frowned. "I'm depending on you, Jessie. What colors do *you* think I'd like to live with?"

No question, his big, empty condo was a clean slate waiting for a woman's touch to soften it and turn it into a home. *Whoa, girl.* He needed a child-friendly home, but a masculine, bachelor one. Not one with her stamp on it. His place could never be hers. And neither could the man.

Nibbling her lower lip, she did her best to reach for any knowledge she might have once possessed to get herself started. She remembered one of the most important things in decorating a client's space was providing a reflection of that client. She knew Peter better than she'd ever know a client. Undoubtedly the problem. Or was it? If she got her act together, maybe it could be the solution. "I think you'd like to live with warm colors."

"Warm colors?" He sounded vaguely interested.

She tried to envision colors that reflected him. "Warm browns to tie in with the wood floors. Orange— no—red accents, I think. Red is stronger, more powerful. And maybe…bronze metals?"

He squinted as if he couldn't understand how she'd ever come up with such a harebrained scheme.

She tried to calm her panic. "Do you hate it?"

A slow smile softened his face. "Warm, strong, powerful? Sounds good."

Warm, strong and powerful. That was the way she saw him. With a few additions. But his flicker of interest spurred her imagination. "Do we have the colors, then?"

He gave a nod.

Yes! "Then let's talk about style preferences."

"I'm sure it will come as no surprise that I don't know one style from the other."

Of course he didn't. She scanned furniture displays near them, a particular sofa snagging her attention. "Do you want to see if we can find a clean-lined, comfortable couch that's perfect for you?"

"Absolutely. Lead on."

She smiled, relieved he still had faith in her despite last night. How could she not feel good about that? For the first time today, she was beginning to have a little faith in herself. Maybe she really could help him with his condo after all.

Standing in Karen and Scott's small foyer with Jessie and Jake, the pride in Peter's chest managed to eclipse the hurt and disappointment he still felt after Jessie's rejection last night. He couldn't remember ever feeling so proud. He hadn't realized how much he'd been looking forward to this moment.

"He looks even more like his daddy than in the pictures you showed us, Peter." Masking her obvious fatigue with a smile, Karen clasped Jessie's hand. "It's good to finally meet you."

Jessie smiled. "And you. Peter's told me so much about you and Scott."

"He's waiting for us in the sunroom." Karen led the way through their tiny, cluttered living room and into the airy sunroom.

"Well, hello." Paler than usual, Scott sat in his recliner, a blanket tucked around his legs in spite of the warm room.

Worry gnawed the edges of Peter's mind. Unfortunately, whether the new drug would help Scott or not was still in the if column.

Jessie bent to look into Scott's eyes. "I'm so glad to meet you," she said sincerely.

Scott grinned. "The pleasure's mine, Jessie."

Peter's throat was so tight, all he could do was beam down at them. He'd known Scott and Karen would love Jessie. What wasn't to love?

Jessie straightened and smiled at Peter as if she sensed how much her meeting his friends meant to him. She seemed to understand him on so many levels, it boggled his mind. She liked him, he was sure of it. Just as sure as he was that she'd wanted him to kiss her last night…almost as much as he'd wanted to kiss her. But then, he reminded himself, she'd played her just-friends card.

Trouble was, he was pretty much past the just-friends stage of their relationship.

"And who's this handsome little guy?" Scott focused on Jake. "Can it be Jake?"

Jake solemnly studied Scott.

"I can see you're sizing me up. Smart boy." Scott met Peter's eyes. "He's amazing, Peter."

Peter grinned, his heart full enough to burst.

Karen motioned to the settee flanking Scott's chair.

Peter sat down and settled Jake on his lap.

Jessie sat beside them.

Doing his best to distract himself from her closeness, Peter dug a little car from his pocket and handed it to Jake.

"Car." Jake held it up for Scott and Karen to see.

"Very nice," Scott said on a chuckle. "Jessie, I hope you made Peter buy something for that big empty condo of his."

Jessie laughed. "We almost bought out the store."

"You're a shopping dynamo." Peter smiled at her. "She really knows what she's doing, too. My place is going to be terrific."

"I'm surprised you got him to look at furniture," Karen said. "But to actually buy some? I'm impressed."

"We bought dishes and glasses. We even bought a couple pans," Peter offered.

"Pans?" Karen raised her eyebrow. "Are you planning to cook?"

"You never know. Actually, I'm hoping Jessie and Jake will be visiting. Often. Jessie knows what to do with pans. And little boys. And decorating." He grinned at her.

She gave him a shy and very charming smile.

"Do you have training in decorating?" Karen asked.

"Some. It was my major in college."

Peter looked at her, surprised. "Then why do you run a diner?"

"Because we already have a decorator in Noah's Crossing who barely gets by. And the diner happened to be for sale when I needed a business."

"I'm surprised you moved to a town where you couldn't put your degree to work for you," Karen said.

"I'd need another year of college to earn my degree. But I needed to go home."

Peter met Jessie's eyes. "Jake entered the picture while she was recovering from injuries from a car accident," he explained.

"Sounds as if you have your hands pretty full," Karen observed.

"Yes," Jessie agreed.

Coughing, Scott reached for a tissue on the table beside him. "Peter talks about you and Jake all the time," he wheezed.

"He's pretty taken with your parents, too," Karen offered. "And your aunts and uncles and cousins."

Jessie laughed. "I suppose he told you, I'm related to half of Noah's Crossing."

"At least," he joked. Things couldn't be going better, could they? "By the way, your Aunt Lou mailed me an invitation to her daughter's wedding next weekend."

"Then you'll meet the entire clan," Jessie said.

He smiled, warmed by her inclusion in a family event despite her reservations about their relationship.

"He's a lot more fun now that he doesn't spend every waking moment in the lab," Scott said. "You and Jake have really opened up his world. Thank you for that, Jessie."

Peter should probably be embarrassed. In truth, he was a lot more curious about how Jessie would respond. He looked at her.

She met his eyes. "He's good for Jake and me, also."

His heart spilled over. Wow. She'd given a better response than he could ever have imagined. He wanted to kiss her on the spot.

But if she felt so good about him, why was she convinced things would go wrong if they got more involved? He just didn't get it. Bending, he retrieved Jake's car from the floor and handed it to his son.

"Tanku." Jake pointed to Peter. "Daddy Pedo."

Goose bumps swarmed Peter's skin. He looked at Jake. Had he called him Daddy?

Jake laughed.

Bursting out laughing, Peter turned to Jessie. "Did you hear him?"

She nodded, tears glistening in her eyes.

He held her gaze, desperately wanting to hug her. Instead, he turned to Karen and Scott. "Did you hear him call me Daddy?"

They smiled. "Loud and clear," Scott said.

Feeling like king of the mountain, Peter stroked his son's head. "I want at least a dozen of these little guys!"

Scott laughed. "I'd love to see that."

Peter gave Jessie a wink.

But she wasn't laughing. She, obviously, didn't think he was nearly as funny as he did.

Jessie lay her head back against the seat as Peter drove away from Scott and Karen's home. "Their courage is so inspiring. They're amazing, Peter."

"Yes."

"I thought I understood your dedication to your research, but meeting Scott and Karen, I understand completely why you're so driven to find answers. You can't give up."

"No," he said quietly.

"And what a wonderful time for Jake to call you Daddy."

Peter laughed. "I couldn't believe it."

She'd been so happy for Peter, so caught up in the moment, his comment about wanting a dozen little guys had stopped her cold. A cruel joke he had no idea he was playing.

But cruel or not, she'd needed the reminder, hadn't she?

"They're just as impressed with you and Jake, you know."

She smiled. "Thank you." She looked around. He seemed to be heading for the interstate, not the car rental place at the airport. "Jake and I are dropping you at the car-rental place, right?"

"I've decided to drive you home."

"What?" She whipped around to look at him. "But you can't. Didn't you say you have work waiting for you at the lab?"

He frowned. "There's no reason you need to worry about driving all that way."

He was putting her and Jake before his work? Her heart stuttered. But she couldn't let him do that. His work was too important. And she was perfectly capable of driving home. Surprisingly, she was actually looking forward to the challenge. Imagine that. "But I'm looking forward to driving your SUV again."

He took his eyes off the road long enough to shoot her a skeptical glance.

"Or maybe you don't trust my driving? Did I fail your driving instruction class this morning?" she asked.

"Of course not."

"Then I promise we'll be fine on the back roads

with your nifty navigator to keep us from getting lost. Honest."

His jaw clenched. "You wouldn't just say that to keep me from making the trip, would you?"

"No. If I was as nervous as I was on the way down, I'd take you up on your offer. But I'm feeling much more confident. Thanks to your encouragement."

"My pleasure. But the credit belongs to you, Jessie."

Of course, he'd say that. "I think Aunt Lou was right. It was good to get away from the normal routine for a couple days. I'd almost forgotten there really is a world outside Noah's Crossing."

He gave her his crooked grin. "Funny how much of my world is centered in Noah's Crossing now. And not only because Jake is there."

She couldn't deny his words warmed her heart. But she had no right to accept them. "Please don't say that, Peter."

"It's the truth."

Heart aching, she wanted to reach out and touch him. Instead, she shook her head and turned to look out the side window. He was the most thoughtful, kind, considerate man on the planet. He made her believe in herself. And the more time she spent with him, the more time she wanted to be with him.

*Oh God, if only I could be the woman he needs.*

But she knew better. Just as she knew she wasn't being fair to Peter by not telling him she could never give him the babies he wanted.

*I should tell him, God. But he never looks at me with pity in his eyes. That will change the minute I tell him. Just like it changed when I told Neil and Clarissa.*

* * *

Peter hovered beside his SUV in the car-rental lot, unwilling to let Jessie and Jake go. "Thanks for your ideas, your help shopping…"

"Did I get too carried away?"

"Are you kidding? I'm really looking forward to the furniture delivery. I'll be able to sit in my living room on something other than that hard, stone hearth."

She smiled. "Are you planning to use your new coffeemaker tomorrow morning?"

"Absolutely. Thanks for setting it up for me."

She smiled. "You're very welcome."

"I'll think of you every time I make a cup of coffee."

"Peter…" Her smile dimmed a little. "I guess I'd better get on the road so I can be home before dark."

"You're sure you don't want me to drive you home?"

"I'm sure."

He blew out a breath, wanting to lean in the window and kiss her goodbye. Unfortunately, she'd drawn the line at friendship. He looked at Jake sound asleep in his car seat in the back. "You should have a quiet ride, at least for a while."

"I'll keep him safe, Peter. I promise."

"You stay safe, too, Jessie." Needing to touch her, he reached through the window and laid his hand on her shoulder.

She gave him a hesitant smile. "You, too."

"I've loved having you and Jake here."

"It's been fun." She started the car.

He withdrew his hand.

With a wave, she drove away.

It felt like the sun went out.

The two people who gave him so much to smile about

every single day were on their way to Noah's Crossing. Away from him.

Why hadn't he insisted on driving them home?

He blew out a breath. Jessie had wanted to drive, and he'd wanted to encourage her. But a car accident could happen to anyone. In the blink of an eye.

And what about deer? Why hadn't he thought about deer? Dusk always brought out several that had no compunction about jumping into a car's path.

He'd never worried much about people before, except for Scott. He had the feeling worry was the downside of caring. He remembered Jessie offering to pray for Scott and him. Maybe he should give it a try.

But what should he say? What did one say to the Supreme Being who'd created everything, including him? Should he assume God knew him? Maybe. Didn't He know everything and everybody?

Peter cleared his throat as if he was about to give a speech. He'd laugh at himself if this wasn't such serious business. *Uh, God...this is Peter...Sheridan. I'm new at this...but I guess you know that. I have an important request. Hope that's okay my first time out of the gate. I'd like you to watch out for Jessie and Jake and keep them safe. Thank you.*

Only God knew if he'd done it right. Shaking his head, he strode for the airport terminal to pick up his car. *By the way, God, I'm not asking because I think I deserve consideration. But because Jessie and Jake do.*

# Chapter Fourteen

Needing to burn off energy, Jessie rolled paint on the bedroom wall she'd left unfinished the night Peter showed up unexpectedly. She'd called him as soon as she'd pulled into her parents' driveway to let him know they'd arrived ahead of the rain she'd heard of on a radio forecast.

She thought about the tension in his voice. About his relief that she and Jake were safely home. He cared about Jake…and her, too, as deeply and thoroughly as he did everything else.

She sighed, refusing to get snagged on problems nibbling the edges of her mind. Her time in Madison with Peter had been unbelievable, wonderful, life-changing. She felt almost invincible. Almost free from the awful things that had held her down and kept her a victim since the accident. She wanted to shout from the roof-tops. "Jessica Louise Chandler is back, baby!"

She laughed at herself. *Well, at least, maybe I'm getting there. Thanks to Peter.*

Pounding on the downstairs door startled her. Somebody was always dropping in, which is why she usually left it unlocked. But Peter had been on her mind so much tonight, she'd heeded his warning and locked it. She laid the paint roller in the tray and hurried down to open the door.

"Since when do you keep the place locked up like a fortress?" Maggie pushed her way inside. "It's raining cats and dogs out there. Good thing we cancelled our walk, but I had to find out how things went in Madison."

Of course she did. "Everything went great."

"Yeah?"

Jessie nodded. "I'm painting."

"That's what you said in your message. I wore old clothes so I can help you while you fill me in." Maggie bounced up the steps. "Your bedroom?"

"Yep." Jessie trotted up the stairs behind her.

Maggie rushed into the bedroom. "Where—never mind. I see your supply corner."

Jessie picked up her roller and continued painting where she'd left off.

"We'll have this room finished in no time." Maggie grasped the paint can, poured paint into a tray, grabbed a roller and began painting. "Okay, spill everything."

"Where should I start?"

"That good? No nightmares after seeing the accident scene, then?"

"Actually, Peter turned off the interstate and took back roads before we got to the place the accident happened."

"Did you tell him it was coming up?"

"Yes."

"He was that sensitive to how you felt?" Maggie sounded doubtful.

"He's won—" Jessie swallowed. "He's a good man, Maggie. You've seen how he is with Jake."

"Yes, I have. I've seen how he is with you, too."

Jessie frowned over her shoulder at her friend. "What's that mean?"

"He likes you."

"I like him, too. We're friends." Jessie began painting the final wall.

"You seem...different."

"How?"

"I don't know. Happy, I think."

Jessie laughed. "Maggie...I drove Jake and me home. I took back roads instead of the interstate, but I'm feeling pretty good about it, just the same."

"You said you'd take the bus. That's a big deal, Jess. Congratulations."

She grinned. "Thanks."

"Was your driving Peter's idea?" Maggie asked.

"The whole trip was his idea. If he hadn't convinced me to help him figure out what to do with his new condo, I would never have gone. I'm so glad I did."

"So the condo thing went okay?"

"We ended up buying quite a few pieces of furniture."

Maggie rolled on paint, apparently lost in thought for several minutes. "You know...Peter's beginning to sound like he might be good for you. Maybe I was a tad hasty in judging him. Maybe he'll help you finally get over Neil."

Neil was part of that awful time in her life she was putting behind her. A part of the reason she'd felt like such a victim. "I'm over him." Saying the words gave her a sense of relief.

"Are you, Jess?"

"Most definitely," she said with conviction.

"About time." Maggie heaved a disgusted sigh. "Then

I can tell you, he wasted no time in moving on. Wife, baby, the whole nine yards."

"His parents told my parents that he had a baby. I hope he's very happy. I really do." She shot a slant-eyed look at Maggie. "But you should talk about finally moving on. You're still pining away for a guy you haven't seen for how many years?"

"Hey, do I look like I'm pining away?"

"Just proves you've had a lot of practice hiding your feelings, that's all."

"Hey, we're talking about you."

Jessie stopped painting and turned to her friend. "I vote we talk about you."

"No way. Your life is a lot more interesting." Maggie went right on painting. "Will asked me what I know about Peter. I think he's feeling protective. And threatened."

Maggie in determined mode was tough to ignore. Jessie went back to rolling on paint. "You know very well Will's a good friend. And I've always been straight with him."

"Yeah, I know." Maggie sighed again. "It's too bad we can't always control who we fall in love with, isn't it?"

Jessie gave her friend a sympathetic look. Maggie would swear she wasn't in love with Tony, but Jessie knew better. A sliver of apprehension shivered through her. Of course she wasn't falling in love with Peter.

Was she?

She shook her head. That couldn't be what was happening to her. Falling in love with him would be irresponsible. Even masochistic. He wanted babies she couldn't give him. Falling in love with him would make their arrangement with Jake impossible.

She could never let that happen.

If only she could share her thoughts and feelings with Maggie like she used to before the accident. It would be so good to be able to talk this through and get her no-nonsense advice.

But to do that, she'd have to tell Maggie the extent of her injuries. What good would that do? Maggie was feeling happy for her for the first time in so long. Telling her would only make Jessie a victim all over again.

Organ music swelled in grandeur. Peter watched bridesmaids in blue slowly make their way up the flower-lined aisle in the packed church on Noah's Crossing's Main Street.

All dressed up in a dark blue outfit with short pants, Jake sat on Peter's lap, wide-eyed and curious. Suddenly, he pointed. "Mama!"

Jessie's parents and several relatives around them murmured in amusement.

Peter spotted Jessie strolling up the aisle in an off-the-shoulder dress that flowed over her soft curves like spun silk. She'd swept her hair off her neck and pinned a white flower in it. She was stunning. A rush of pride poured through him.

Walking past their pew, Jessie smiled at Jake, her face soft with love.

Peter's breath caught even when he knew all that love was directed at Jake, not him. He couldn't remember anybody ever looking at him that way.

"Mama!" Jake's tiny arms shot into the air. "Hole me, 'kay?"

Jessie's parents chuckled along with others around them.

Peter grinned proudly. Jake was, obviously, a big hit with Jessie's entire family.

"Mama!"

Jessie caught Peter's eye with a meaningful look that said, "You're in charge, so handle this."

Whoops. Obviously, not a good time for Jake to steal the show. He gave her a nod. Now all he had to do was to live up to the responsibility. Dragging his gaze from her, he remembered the trains in his tux pocket. He dug one out and showed the tiny, green engine to Jake.

"No train. Mama."

"Later," Peter whispered in his small ear.

Jake shook his head, his bottom lip protruding. "Now, Daddy Pedo."

Peter couldn't help chuckling every time the little guy called him Daddy. And Daddy Peter cracked him up. But his chuckle died the moment he remembered the storm Jake's protruding bottom lip usually signaled. Hurriedly, he dragged another engine out of his pocket and ran it along Jake's arm to distract him.

"No." Jake shook his head, his little face scrunching as if he was seriously working himself into tears. "No, no, no, no," he chanted in time to his shaking head.

Beside him, Mrs. Chandler laid her hand on Jake's knee and lifted one finger to her lips.

"No," Jake said loudly. "Wan' Mama."

Mrs. Chandler stroked Jake's leg and smiled at Peter.

Smile or not, he got the same message Jessie's look had conveyed. Handle it.

Oh, boy. Neither Jessie nor her parents nor anybody else in the church would be impressed if Jake ruined the wedding by having a meltdown. Going for broke, Peter pulled the last train out of his pocket and held it up for Jake to see.

"Tomut." Jake took the little Thomas engine and scrambled to get down to play.

Peter started to set him on the floor, then had second thoughts. Jake running loose in the church? Probably not such a good idea. He turned the little guy to stand in his lap.

"Down, Daddy Pedo."

Thankfully, the organ shifted into full volume.

Jake looked around as everybody stood and turned toward the aisle.

Peter lifted Jake and climbed to his feet, catching a glimpse of the bride strolling up the aisle on Harold's arm.

Making a low chugging sound, Jake ran the train along Peter's shoulder, up his neck and across his forehead.

Peter turned to look for Jessie.

Six bridesmaids stood in a line at the front of the flower-laden church. All were in medium blue dresses, blond tresses swept up and adorned with a single white blossom. He recognized Lisa from the diner, her slim figure thickening with her pregnancy. But his gaze homed in on Jessie.

She met his eyes and gave him a nervous little smile.

Peering around Jake's busy hands running his train over his face, Peter grinned as if she'd granted him the highest possible honor. Hadn't she acknowledged him in a church filled with relatives and people she'd known her entire life? He couldn't take his eyes off her even when she turned as the bride and groom moved in front of the altar and the congregation sat down.

He sat, too, alternating between watching Jessie and doing his best to keep Jake quietly amused while the ceremony spun out. He listened to the solos and the minister's short sermon about the sacredness of marriage, then they got to the vows. "Promise to love… honor…cherish…in sickness and health…'til death do us part."

What an extraordinary commitment. One he'd never been tempted to make, had wondered if he ever would.

But Jessie was all about love and deep commitment. She was about family, too, one with lots of kids and love and time for each other. The kind of family he'd realized he wanted since knowing Jake and Jessie.

Applause erupted, startling him.

The organ jolted to life with celebratory music. The bride and groom practically ran down the aisle, laughing and exuberant.

"Mama!" Jake pointed.

Smiling at Jake, Jessie hurried by on some guy's arm, her eyes glistening with tears.

Peter's heart clenched. He wanted to wipe away her tears. And he wanted her on *his* arm. Not some other guy's.

A vision of her all in white popped into his mind's eye. He mulled over the thought of Jessie as a bride. Not just anybody's bride.

His bride. His wife.

Of her not only Jake's mother, but the mother of children they'd have together. Children they could share from the beginning. The thought of Jessie's body swollen with his baby growing inside her made him smile.

He liked the idea. He liked it a lot.

Because when all was said and done, his accomplishments and contributions were only part of his worth, weren't they? They weren't his entire reason for being.

He was beginning to see Jessie and Jake were meant to be in his life.

Which went way beyond the friendship Jessie insisted she wanted. He had to find a way to calm her fears and convince her that if she took a chance on him, he'd never let her down. What better time to get through to her than when her thoughts were on weddings?

Problem was he'd need to get her alone, which was not easy with relatives swarming everywhere. But he'd find a way. And when he did, he knew just the secluded spot he wanted to take her.

The wedding dinner seemed to drag on forever with Jessie at the head table and Peter struggling with a tired Jake at a table with her parents and relatives. Finally, Peter took him back to the house and left him with the sitter Jessie had arranged. Luckily, he returned to the community hall in time to get a piece of the amazing strawberry-cream wedding cake Jessie had made for her cousin.

Now, he stood beside her, watching many of her relatives and friends dancing an enthusiastic hop polka. Jessie had told him that the Buttons and Banjo band played great dancing music. The noise level was deafening right now, though. Concertina, banjo, tuba and drums competed with most of the residents of Noah's Crossing talking and laughing. He wondered how long it would be before he'd find the opportunity he needed to be alone with Jessie.

"Welcome to a wedding dance, Noah's Crossing style," she yelled so he could hear her above the din.

He bent his head closer to her ear. "Looks like fun.

Do you think you can teach me how to do that?" He motioned to the dancers on the floor.

She shook her head. "Too dangerous out there."

He grinned. "I hear danger can sometimes be fun."

She pointed to her feet in their strappy, towering heels. "Killing me."

"Those look lethal. Why don't you take them off?" He motioned to the girls and women dancing in their bare or stocking feet.

She shook her head. "These are the first heels I've bought since the accident. Probably not the sanest thing I've ever done. I'll probably be paying for my mistake for days, but aren't they gorgeous?"

He laughed. "I never figured you for a beauty-at-all-costs kind of girl."

"I couldn't spoil the outfit, now, could I?"

"There you are, Peter." Jessie's mother clasped his hand. "I want you to meet my brother Stan."

Peter gave Liz a warm smile. She and Max had been busy introducing him to one relative after another all day. Sure was great to be on their good side. He turned and shook Stan's hand. "Nice to meet you. I assume you saw Jessie's cake?"

Jessie rolled her eyes at Peter. "I'm pleased you liked my cake, but bringing it up to everybody you meet is getting a little embarrassing."

"I can't help it." He cocked an eyebrow. "It was the most beautiful, best-tasting cake I've ever eaten."

Stan gave her an a-ok sign. "He's right, Jess. Don't tell Delores I had two pieces."

Jessie put her finger to her lips.

Stan turned to Jessie's mom. "Would you like to dance, little sis?"

"Absolutely." Liz led the way.

Stan followed. "Nice meeting you, Peter."

"Same here." Peter glanced around. No impending relatives in sight. As good a time as any to steal Jessie away.

"Are you enjoying the dance, Peter?"

Foiled again. Peter almost groaned, but Maggie looked at him as if she might want to be friends. A pleasant surprise. "Good to see you, Maggie. How about Jessie's cake? Amazing, wasn't it?"

Jessie groaned. "You're impossible."

"She has many talents." Maggie smiled. "Speaking of one of her talents, are you enjoying your new furniture?"

"Very much."

"Uh-oh. Heads up, Jess." With a giggle, Maggie grabbed Jessie's arm. "Lou's heading straight for us. You know what that means."

"Oh, no. The dreaded bouquet toss." Jessie looked around as if she wanted to run away.

Peter would be more than happy to go with her.

"Sorry, kiddo. I'm opting out of this one. You're on your own." Maggie took off as if she'd been shot from a cannon.

"Where's Maggie off to?" Lou asked. "Mary's about ready to throw her bouquet."

"That's for the younger women, Aunt Lou."

"Fiddlesticks," Lou yelled over the racket. "Donna Cleveland is seventy-four and she's always out there."

"If you have your way, you'll have me trying to catch the bouquet when I'm seventy-four, too."

"Let's hope it doesn't take that long, dear." Glancing at Peter, Lou projected her voice over the noise. "Sorry, Peter. I need to borrow Jess for a few minutes."

Borrow? Jessie's aunt thought she needed to *borrow*

Jessie from him? As if they were a couple? He'd always liked Lou.

"Jess, this time, at least *try* to catch it," Lou admonished.

"Listen up, folks," the tuba player announced. "The bride's mother has asked me to announce that the bride is ready to throw her bouquet to one of you lucky single ladies out there. So if you're hoping to be next to waltz down that aisle, make your way to the front of the room as fast as you can."

Peter liked the tradition behind catching the bouquet. But Jessie looked as if she needed rescuing. Anyway, she didn't need to catch that bouquet. He had a better idea. He draped a possessive arm around her shoulders. "I'm sorry, Lou, but Jessie and I were just going to take a little stroll."

Jessie gave him a surprised look.

"Oh?" Lou's eyebrows shot up.

"I'm sure you understand," Peter said. "With all the festivities today, I haven't seen much of her."

Lou smiled. "You just take your time on that stroll, Peter."

A woman after his own heart. "Thank you. We will." Peter's arm firmly around Jessie, he escorted her through the crowd.

Jessie laughed up at him. "Thank you, I think. But you do know that Aunt Lou is telling everybody what you said, don't you?"

He was counting on it. He pushed through the door and out into the cool night air.

"Ahh, freedom." Jessie took a breath and rubbed her bare arms as if she was chilled.

Peter shrugged off his tux jacket and gently draped it around her shoulders.

"Thank you."

"You're very welcome." He bent and swept her off her feet.

"What are you doing?" she sputtered.

He liked having her in his arms. "What does it look like I'm doing? I'm carrying you. I figure the last thing you need in those shoes is a stroll."

"My feet thank you. But just where are you carrying me?"

"To a nice, quiet place." Striding with purpose, he left the sidewalk and walked across soft grass into a little woods that smelled of earth and green things.

She relaxed against him.

Her trust made him feel strong and powerful and more in charge than he usually felt around her. He had so much to say to her, he wasn't sure where to begin. Before long, the small, white gazebo took shape in the dim light of the waning moon.

"You found the gazebo?"

"Jake and I found it one day when we were playing in the park." He climbed several steps and set her down on one of the plank benches hugging the enclosure. Missing her closeness, he sat beside her. "This is nice," he said. Very private, too. A perfect spot to tell her how he felt. "Being near you makes me happy, Jessie."

She smiled. "Thank you."

Moving closer, he took her hand and looked into her eyes. "When I go back to Madison without you, I feel empty. I miss your warmth, your vulnerability, your strength. I'd rather be with you than anywhere else on earth."

She opened her mouth as if to say something.

"Please hear me out." He caressed her cheek. "You're the most giving person I've ever known. You could have easily led Jake to mistrust me, but you helped me win his trust instead. When I went off on a self-serving tangent to take him to live with me, you forgave me. You've taken me into your family as if I belong. You've given me so much, Jessie. No wonder I've fallen in love with you."

Her eyes went wide.

Leaning toward her, he cupped her neck with his fingers and gently coaxed her to meet him halfway.

She didn't pull away.

Heart pounding, he hesitantly kissed her jaw, her chin. Little puffs of her sweet breath warming him, he carefully kissed one corner of her mouth, then the other. She tasted of strawberry punch.

She lifted her chin as if offering more.

It was all the encouragement he needed. He fit his mouth over hers. Waited for what he wasn't sure would happen.

With a sigh, she kissed him back.

He couldn't catch his breath. Needing to be closer, he gently drew her into his embrace. Her lemon scent wafted around him like a cocoon. Soft, warm, inviting. He drank her in like a man dying of thirst. The last thing he wanted was to end the kiss.

But that's what he needed to do if he was going to tell her all he had to say. Lifting his head, he smiled at her.

She looked a little stunned.

He felt a little stunned himself. And more alive than he'd ever felt in his life. "I love you. And I want to marry you as soon as we can get a license."

"Oh, Peter." Tears sparkled in her eyes. "You want a family."

"Absolutely. Won't it be great? You, me, Jake and a

whole bunch just like him? I can't wait to experience all the firsts together. You're such a good mother. I promise we'll have as many playmates for Jake as you want to have."

She gave her head a little shake and looked away.

"I think of you always, Jessie. Of the way you are with our son. The way I feel when I see you again. It's like coming home for the first time in my life."

He tipped her chin so she had to look at him. "A significant grant came through recently that will allow me to hire another full-time researcher. I'll cut back on hours. I'll learn to delegate more responsibilities and use the computer to stay on top of things at the lab. I'll do whatever it takes to spend more time in Noah's Crossing with you and Jake. Will you marry me, Jessie?"

# *Chapter Fifteen*

Jessie's heart thudded against her ribs. She wanted to stay in his arms forever. He'd just laid his heart at her feet, and she wanted so badly to accept it. She desperately wanted to be the woman he needed.

But she couldn't. And now, she'd hurt him by not being honest about who she was.

Her chest felt so heavy, she could barely breathe. *Why didn't I tell him, God? I was so caught up protecting myself, I didn't think about him.* Closing her eyes to shut out the warmth in Peter's gaze, she pulled away. "I can't marry you."

He frowned.

"I tried to tell you that night in Madison…friends is all we can ever be."

He blew out a breath. "You don't feel about me the way I feel about you?"

"That's not it." A sob shook her.

Smiling, he brushed tears from her cheek. "Then we can fix anything else."

"No, Peter. We can't." Tears blinded her.

"Don't worry about leaving everybody you love, Jessie. You and Jake can continue living in Noah's

Crossing if you want. Tell me what you need. Anything. We'll work it out." He looked at her as if he'd do whatever she said.

She couldn't stand it. "I'm not all you think I am, Peter."

"You're everything I want."

"I wish I was," she said sadly. "But wishing will never make it true."

He shook his head. "What are you talking about?"

The only way he could understand is if she told him the truth. She tried to figure out what words to use. Words that would shatter his belief in her as a woman and make him look at her with pity.

She couldn't do it. She had to get out of here. She got to her feet.

"Don't you think I deserve to know what bothers you about me?" Peter stood and handed her his handkerchief.

She mopped her face with it. "Nothing bothers me about you," she said honestly.

"Then why can't you tell me why you think a relationship between us is impossible? Why can't you trust me enough to open up?"

"It's not a matter of trusting you."

"Then what is it a matter of, Jessie?"

She didn't want to answer. She wanted so badly to run away. Away from her feelings for him. Away from her lack of courage. Away from the pain of having to voice her biggest disappointment out loud. If only his words didn't sing through her mind like a beautiful love song. *You've given me so much, Jessie. It's no wonder I've fallen in love with you.*

Words she'd remember forever, but words he'd said because she hadn't told him why he couldn't love her.

Fighting more tears, shame washed over her. He'd asked her a fair question. When was she going to stop running away from him and give him a fair answer?

"I…should have told you—" She pressed her fingers to her lips, but she made herself go on. "Something very important. I'm so sorry."

He wound his fingers through hers. "Tell me now."

Her mind shot back to the pain in Neil's eyes when she'd told him. Even then, she'd thought they could get through it, get married as planned, adopt babies.

But the loss was too great for him to overcome.

Just as it would be too great for Peter.

*I've put off telling him too long. Dear God, please help me tell him the truth now.*

She dropped her gaze to their clasped hands, unwilling to watch the admiration in his eyes turn to disappointment and pity. "My injuries…from the accident…I didn't tell you everything. I…didn't tell you…I can never have a baby." Her voice sounded so matter-of-fact. As if her heart wasn't crumbling in a million tiny pieces.

He stared at her as if trying to digest what she'd said.

She saw disappointment in his eyes. She'd expected it and there it was. But why wouldn't he be disappointed? She gave him a half-hearted smile. "I know how much you want more babies. And you should have them."

Without a word, he wrapped her close.

She reached her arms around his waist, grateful his warmth and strength gave her courage to go on. "That's why Neil broke off the engagement and moved away. Leaving was the only way he could deal with everything. I wasn't able to deal with it at all. I couldn't understand why God spared me from my injuries only to take away my future. I never told anyone except Neil and Clarissa."

He stroked her back.

It was as if once she began, she had to tell him everything. "If Clarissa hadn't come home pregnant and asked me to adopt her baby, I don't know how I would have survived. But when I watched Jake come into the world and held him when he was only minutes old, I finally knew I'd be okay."

He kissed the top of her head, supportive as always.

But she could hear his heart pounding in his chest, feel the tension in his arms. Her world crashing around her, she backed away.

He clasped her hand. Pain in his eyes, he shook his head. "I had no idea, Jessie. You're such a great mother. It's so unfair."

She nodded.

He squeezed her hand. "Don't think for one second this changes how I feel about you."

"It will when you've had time to think about it."

"I love you. Whether you can have a baby or not doesn't matter."

Her heart breaking, she held up her hand. "I know you too well to believe that, Peter. Please don't say any more. Please, leave. I need to be alone."

He frowned. "I'm not Neil. I won't leave you. Don't shut me out again."

She pressed her fingers to her mouth to stifle a sob. "I have to." Wrenching her hand free, she turned her back on him. She struggled to hold herself together. "Please go. Please, Peter. I need you to leave me alone."

He laid his hand on her shoulder.

She stiffened.

Heaving a sigh, he took his hand away.

Finally, she heard him walk down the path. Felt the emptiness because he wasn't near. The unbearable loneliness. Tears blinding her, she could still see his wonderful, sincere face. Still hear his words as he poured out his heart to her. *I think of you always. Of the way you are with our son. About the way I feel every time I see you again. It's like coming home for the first time in my life.*

How could she be so cruel? He'd never had a home. Never had a family. And he'd believed he'd found one with her.

She closed her eyes. *How could I have done that to him? And how can I get through the evenings if he doesn't call? The weekends without seeing him?*

*I love him, God. He's become such an important part of my life, how can I let him go? Help me to let him go.*


Swatting away the drone of a mosquito in his ear, Peter paced in the little woods near the gazebo. He'd never felt so out of control of a situation in his life.

Jessie still huddled on the gazebo bench, hugging her knees, his tux jacket tenting around her.

He couldn't leave her. He wanted to help her, but how? She didn't want his help. She'd sent him away.

Not that he could blame her.

How many times had he talked about wanting kids? Lots of kids? To her and just about anybody else who'd listen?

The idea of being a father had been so new and exciting to him, he'd gotten carried away. Jessie was such a great mother, he'd assumed *she* wanted a big family. Which, of course, he was sure she did. He closed his eyes against the sharp realization that every time he'd mentioned having kids, he might as well have driven a nail into her heart. How could he have been so dense?

Because having a bunch of kids was…hypothetical. Wasn't it? He blew out a breath. Maybe not so hypothetical after all. He wanted kids with Jessie in a very big way. How could he come to terms with never sharing the intimacies of her pregnancy? Of never marveling with her at the miracle of the birth of their child? Would he ever stop regretting they could never share those things? Jessie had never stopped regretting. Now, he understood that special sadness about her.

His cell vibrated in his pocket.

He didn't want to talk to anybody. But he mechanically retrieved his cell and read the ID. Scott? "This is Peter," he said into the phone.

"It's Karen. I'm following an ambulance with Scott inside."

He tensed. "What happened?"

"He can't breathe." Her voice trembled. "Oxygen isn't helping."

Adrenaline pumping, Peter shook his head. "I'm on my way. I'll meet you at the hospital as soon as I can get there."

"Thank you. Please drive safely, Peter." She clicked off.

Shoving his phone in his pocket, he looked for Jessie. He needed to tell her about Scott. But her hunched figure told him it was all she could do right now to deal with her own problems.

He had to go, but he couldn't leave her so upset and alone. With a lingering look at her, he strode to the community center. She needed to be with somebody who loved her, even if she wouldn't let it be him. He pushed into the noisy commotion and scanned the crowd for Jessie's parents.

"Peter? Where's Jess?"

He turned to face Maggie.

She frowned. "What's wrong?

"Have you seen Jessie's parents?" he asked urgently.

Her eyes widened in alarm. "I'll take you to them." She led the way. "Is it Jake?"

"Jake's fine. It's Jessie."

"Jess? Where is she?"

He spotted the Chandlers talking with another couple.

Max looked up, then said something to his wife. With concern on their faces, they hurried to meet him.

Shivering despite having Peter's jacket around her, Jessie hunched in the gazebo, twisting his handkerchief. How could she have been so blind, so self-centered, so stupid to not tell him the truth the second she knew she was attracted to him?

Now, there was just no way to fix the giant mess she'd made of her own life and the lives of those she loved. The balance they'd worked out with Jake was completely shattered. Peter, Jake and her parents would all suffer because of her cowardice.

"Oh, Jess… What happened, dear?"

"Mom?" Fighting through her haze of guilt and regret, Jessie turned to face her mom…dad…and Maggie striding up the gazebo steps like the cavalry.

Defenses melting in a miserable puddle, Jessie lurched into her mother's outstretched arms. "I can't have a baby. The accident…" she sobbed. Unable to stop words spilling over each other in a rush, Jessie's relief built as she told her parents and Maggie everything she'd been withholding. When she had no more words, her mom guided her to the bench and settled beside her.

"I'm so sorry, sweetheart." Taking her hand, her mom looked at her with all the concern Jessie had grown to hate.

Now she soaked it in like a sponge.

Grasping Jessie's hand, Maggie settled on her other side, her face bathed in tears. "That's why you've been so sad."

Jessie's dad knelt in front of her. "Is that why you haven't dated?"

Jessie bit her lip. "Any man would have to love Jake, Dad. And if he loved Jake, he'd want his own children, too."

Her mom frowned. "Have you told Peter?"

Peter. Tears filled Jessie's eyes. She'd never forget the pain on his face. "Yes. Tonight."

"Oh." Mom looked at Dad. "I thought he was upset because—"

"He asked us to tell you he had to rush back to Madison," her dad said. "His friend was taken to the hospital."

"Oh, no." Jessie shook her head. Poor Peter. "What happened to Scott?"

"Peter didn't elaborate. Just told us you were in the gazebo and you needed us." Her dad cleared his throat.

Her heart stuttered. She'd sent Peter away, and even with Scott in trouble, he was trying to take care of her.

"When you told him," Maggie narrowed her eyes, "what did he say?"

"He said it doesn't matter."

Maggie took a quick breath. "Hallelujah. Oh, Jess, I'm so glad he's turning out to be one of the good ones."

"You don't understand. Having a baby matters, Maggie. It matters to me and I know it matters to Peter, whether he says so or not."

"Having a baby *is* a huge deal, Jess," Maggie said quietly. "What I meant is Peter was supportive when you told him. Maybe the two of you can adopt."

"If only it was that simple," Jessie said.

Maggie gripped Jessie's hand hard. "Anything about a baby is never simple, Jess," she whispered as if she knew.

But she didn't know. How could she? She'd never had a baby, and she wouldn't know how a man felt about the matter either. Jessie looked to her dad. "You wanted your own babies, right, Dad?"

"Truthfully, I didn't put much thought into it, Jess."

Jessie shook her head. "But being a father is more important to you than any other dad I know."

Her mom patted Jessie's hand. "When your dad graduated from college, he was headed to the naval academy right after summer vacation." She gave Dad a little smile. "He wanted to test airplanes, the kind that take off and land on a ship."

"But I wanted your mother more. We ended up getting pregnant that summer."

What? A chill shook her. Shouldn't she have known this? She frowned at her dad. "You gave up a military career to get married because Mom was pregnant with us?"

"We loved each other," Mom said. "I'm sure it's hard to hear your parents could have used better judgment.

But we couldn't have been more thankful God gave us you and Clarissa."

"And being married wouldn't have stopped me from a career in the military," her dad explained. "Truth is, I thrived on the risk. But that didn't seem so important anymore with a baby on the way. Well, two babies, it turned out. I wouldn't have missed you and Clarissa growing up for the world."

Jessie's heart hurt. "Dad, we were so important to you, you gave up your plans to be a test pilot. You wouldn't have done that for babies that weren't your own."

Dad frowned, considering her words and apparently unable to refute them. "I think Peter cares too much for you to let it matter that you can't have a baby."

But having a baby mattered. Why couldn't anybody understand how much it mattered? "He deserves to have his own babies. Why should he settle for less?"

"Oh, Jess." Her mom shook her head. "No man in his right mind would think he was settling if he had you. Don't you know how wonderful you are?"

Jessie shot her mom a look. "You're my mother. Of course you think that."

"It's not the only reason, dear. I've prayed for wonderful things for you your whole life, and God always answers my prayers."

"Your mom's right," Maggie said. "I've known since I was about two that Jessica Chandler was the twin with the heart. The one who'd give me a hug when I fell on the playground. The one who'd cry with me when my kitty died. The one who'd chew me out for goofing up, then follow with a silly grin."

Tearing up again, Jessie squeezed her friend's hand. "Stop it. You're making me cry."

"My point is I haven't forgotten who you are…even if *you* have. You're terrific. The real deal. That's what Peter sees if he's as smart as I think he is. So don't give us any more of that settling stuff."

Her dad gave her the look that made her feel like a kid again. "You don't trust Peter."

Jessie frowned. Peter had accused her of not trusting him, too. "How can you say that? Of course I trust him."

Her dad held her gaze. "I don't think you've trusted anybody. Certainly not Maggie, or your mother and me."

She shook her head. "That's not true."

"Then why have you kept this big secret locked inside you for so long?"

"When I told Neil and Clarissa they were so disappointed and upset, I just couldn't do that to you and mom or you, either, Maggie. You were all so worried about me as it was."

"You could have told us, sweetheart," Mom said.

Clearly, she'd made people she loved think she didn't trust them. She'd hurt them. "I'm so sorry I hurt all of you."

Her dad sighed. "You hurt yourself most of all. It's not good to keep everything inside."

She nodded. "After my injuries and the thing with Neil, everybody treated me like such a victim, I couldn't stand it. Clarissa's death made it even worse."

"People care about you, Jess," Mom said.

"But so much concern makes me feel like nobody thinks I can take care of myself anymore," Jessie admitted.

Maggie squinted. "Nobody thinks that. You've

been nothing short of amazing after all you've been through."

"Thank you." Jessie tried to smile, but her heart wasn't in it. "I don't know what I'd do without you guys."

Her mom hugged her. "I'll pray for you and Peter and Jake, dear."

"Thanks, Mom."

"For the record, we couldn't be prouder of you or the way you've handled yourself. Never doubt that, Jess." Her dad gave her a hug, then stood and exchanged looks with his wife and Maggie. "Let's leave Jessie to her thoughts. Jess, when you're ready to go home, take the van. We'll get a ride."

"Thank you." She hugged Maggie and they all left. Pulling Peter's jacket around her, his scent offered her a measure of comfort. She watched a lone firefly float around the gazebo as if it was as lost as she was.

Had she really been trying to protect people she loved from worrying about her? Was that why she hadn't told them? Or had she been protecting herself? She let her mind drift back to all the things she'd faced after the accident.

She'd lost so much. The use of her legs for a while. Her dream of having a baby. Neil. Then Clarissa.

She closed her eyes against the truth. Her dad was right. She hadn't trusted anybody. Was it because she'd told Neil, and he'd let her down? She didn't think so. She wasn't angry with Neil for that. She understood he couldn't have done anything else. No, it wasn't Neil she'd blamed for letting her down, was it?

She'd blamed God.

All those losses had made her distrust God. And if

she couldn't trust Him, no wonder she couldn't trust anyone else.

She bowed her head. *Father, please forgive me. I've made everything so much harder than it had to be, haven't I? If I'd trusted You, would I have seen past my fears of losing Jake when You sent Peter into our lives? Would I have been so terrified of the mere thought of loving Peter? Would I have had the courage to be honest about who I am right from the beginning?*

*Where has all that fear and distrust gotten me? I love him, but I was so afraid of losing him, I kept the truth from him.*

*I've lost him anyway.*

*And I hurt him horribly. I'm so sorry.*

Dawn was beginning to peek through the hospital windows as Peter ducked into the curtain-shrouded, glass cubicle of Scott's intensive care unit. The small space smelled as if it could use a breath of fresh air. *He* sure could.

Eyes closed, Scott looked drawn and pale, but he wasn't fighting for every breath like he had been all night.

Peter had just come from a phone consultation with Scott's doctors. Unfortunately, they'd all agreed the experimental drug they'd been pinning their hopes on had to be stopped.

Failing was bad enough even when it didn't affect somebody Peter loved. But failing Scott was unbearable on so many levels. And even worse, he needed to tell Scott the bad news.

Scott moaned in his sleep.

Peter touched his friend's face. Still clammy.

"How goes it?" Scott kept his eyes closed.

Peter dragged a breath. "Looks like you're kicking the pneumonia."

"Good news."

"Great news, I'd say."

Scott squinted up at him. "I bet you look worse than I do."

"Thanks." Peter sighed. "I'm sorry I wasn't here when they brought you in."

Scott frowned. "You're not responsible for me, Peter."

"I'm partially responsible for taking care of you." Throat closing, Peter laid his hand over his heart. "I'm responsible here."

Tears filled Scott's eyes. "You have a life now. Do you know how much joy that gives me? How's Jake?"

"He's great."

"Jessie?"

Peter flinched without meaning to.

"What's wrong?"

Peter shook his head, unwilling to discuss private issues between him and Jessie. The vision of her huddled in the gazebo would haunt him forever. And he was still struggling with her admission. Of all the things she could possibly have been withholding from him, being unable to have a baby hadn't even made his list.

"I listen easier than I talk," Scott nudged.

Peter hesitated, but he couldn't remember ever needing to talk to his friend more. And when words began pouring out, he couldn't seem to stop them until he'd pretty much laid out the problem.

His declaration of love. Jessie's insistence there could be nothing between them. Finally, her confession. And her sending him away.

"You love her," Scott said.

"Yes."

"Does she love you?"

"I don't know."

"Seems like it's up to her to make the next move."

"I'm not sure she will."

"Don't sell yourself short. You're turning into quite a charming fellow, you know."

Peter laughed in spite of himself. "Now, that's a resounding endorsement."

"How do you feel about never having that dozen or so little Jakes?"

Peter swallowed. "Disappointed. Angry."

"How are you going to come to terms with it?"

"I honestly don't know."

"Aw, you're awake. What's happening with my two favorite men?" Walking into the room, Karen met Peter's eyes.

"We're doing great, my love." Scott extended his hand for her to grasp.

Maybe not so great. Sadness overwhelming Peter, he had to admit he'd been counting on the drug he'd had a huge part in developing to help Scott as much as Scott and Karen had. He blew out a breath and decided there was no reason to put off laying things on the line now that Karen was here. "I just came from a phone consultation with the doctors."

"And?" Karen prodded.

Peter met her eyes, then Scott's. "They're convinced the experimental drug is too hard on your immune system."

Scott gave a nod. "They're stopping it?"

Karen pressed her fingers to her lips.

"I'm sorry. But I agree with them," Peter said.

Scott closed his eyes. "Thanks for giving it a try. I'm

glad the drug's helping others. Maybe the next one will work for me."

"I hope so," Peter said, the realization hitting him that he no longer had the countless hours for research he'd once had. The countless hours it would take to develop one of the other drugs he'd been working on in time to help Scott.

"Never give up," Scott declared.

"Your motto?" Peter asked through a tight throat.

Scott gave him a tired smile. "Absolutely."

Tears blurring his vision, Peter left Scott in Karen's loving arms and discreetly walked out of the room. In the quiet hall, he leaned against the wall, an avalanche of grief and failure threatening to take him under.

He was losing everybody he cared about. Scott. Karen. Jessie. Even Jake in a way. The pain was overwhelming. He'd done his best and still, he'd failed them all in one way or another. They were in so much pain, and he didn't know how to help them. Right now, he couldn't even help himself.

Jessie's quiet words nudged his mind. *All I was able to do was say God's name…and somehow, He was there. Comforting. Easing the pain. Making me stronger.*

Blowing out a breath, Peter pushed himself off the wall and strode down the hall. He had too much to talk over with God to do it in a hospital corridor.

Reaching his car in the almost-deserted lot, he folded into the seat, pulled the door shut and dropped his head in his hands. *It's Peter Sheridan again, God. I'm not doing so great. I need You to take care of Scott and Karen. And Jake.* His throat felt tight. *And Jessie.*

*And I need You to take care of me. Please show me how to help the people I love. Time is running out for*

*Scott. And I can't devote myself entirely to work on the next drug that could help him. That doesn't mean I won't be dedicated, but Jake only has one dad. Please help me get more comfortable relying on others in the lab to carry a heavier load. Show us and other scientists and labs ways to conquer ALS and diseases like it.*

Jessie…. Her voice played in Peter's memory. *I'm not all you think I am, Peter…I wish I was.*

The truth hit him full force. She didn't feel whole, or worthy of love. An ache settled in Peter's chest. It was so wrong. All of it. The only way Jessie would feel whole was to have a baby. An impossibility. What an excruciating thing for her to live with. *God, I just don't understand why the most loving, compassionate woman I've ever known can't have the baby she wants. How could You let that happen to her?*

He shook his head. He was probably doing this all wrong. Who was he to be asking God questions? Or letting his own frustration enter the mix?

But it was all he could do. At the moment, it was all he was capable of. *It's just that she's wonderful, God. She's everything a woman and mother should be. But You know that. And as imperfect as I am, I thought maybe I could make her happy. But I don't know anymore. I don't know how to help her. But I love her, God. That has to count for something.*

He scrubbed his hand over his face. *If You know me, You know I'm used to calling the shots. But in this, I can't do it. I'm counting on You to lead the way with Jessie.*

# Chapter Sixteen

Jessie struggled to focus on Pastor Nick's sermon, but her mind had its own agenda. Peter had called early this morning to tell her Scott was still in intensive care, but he'd improved enough for Peter to drive to Noah's Crossing for a few hours. He said he needed to talk to her. Alone.

She'd been trying to prepare for seeing him ever since. At best, things between them would be strained. She couldn't expect anything else. Would he be upset? Distant? Would he explain that now that he'd thought things over, he knew she wasn't the one for him? *Oh, please, God, don't let him think he needs to explain.*

And Jake. Her breath caught in her throat. How could they go on sharing their son when they had so much between them they could never share? Peter had wanted partial custody in the beginning. Would he want it now?

She shook her head, unable to think about that possibility.

A stir in the aisle broke through her thoughts. She looked up to see Peter threading his way past people sitting in the pew alongside her with all the intensity she loved about him. But he looked exhausted, unshaven, his white shirt and tux trousers rumpled. He'd probably spent the night in the hospital, then driven all this way to see her. In spite of her anxieties, a smile claimed her from deep inside.

He was here.

She shifted to allow him room beside her.

He met her eyes as he sat down, his gaze taking her in as if he needed to see her as much as she needed to see him. But she'd never seen him so tense. Clasping her hand, he bent to whisper in her ear. "Jessie, we need to talk."

She could hear the strain in his voice. Heart aching, she squeezed his hand to let him know she was glad he was here, no matter what he had to say.

She loved having him beside her in church, even if she'd never know how they got through the rest of the service with the tension stretching between them. But they finally stood for the last hymn. As soon as the final note died away, Peter grasped her hand and took charge.

Guiding her around people, he dodged the line waiting to greet the pastor and took a side door outside. He hurried her through the crowded parking lot. "I left my car at the diner and jogged over."

She realized they were heading for the shortcut through the park. Fearing the worst, the only thought that registered is how lucky she'd worn flat sandals today. She could almost keep up with his long strides.

Entering the shade of the trees, he slowed his pace. "Leaving you last night was the hardest thing I've ever done."

"But you sent Maggie and my parents to take care of me. Thank you."

He nodded.

"Scott is doing better?"

"His immune system can't tolerate the experimental drug."

"Oh, no. I know how hopeful you were."

"Yes." He searched her face. "It was rough telling him this morning."

She nodded her understanding, her throat so tight she could barely breathe.

He stopped walking with a jolt and turned to her. "I can't stop thinking about you. About how much courage it took for you to open up to me last night."

"I'm so sorry I didn't tell you the truth sooner."

Frowning, he reached out and smoothed her hair away from her face. "There's no blame here, Jessie."

"Thank you," she whispered. His forgiveness felt good, but she had a long way to go before she could forgive herself.

"This morning, I remembered what you said about prayer helping you through your pain. I prayed all the way to Noah's Crossing, and I realized I need to be honest about my feelings with you."

The explanation she didn't want. But if he needed to say it, listening was the least she could do. She owed him that and more. She met his eyes. "Go on."

"I never should have said that whether you can have a baby or not doesn't matter to me. It matters a great deal."

Throat closing, she fought not to look away.

"I'm disappointed. And I'm angry you can't have the baby you want so much. *We* want so much. That we can never share something so important to both of us."

She nodded, unable to say anything.

"I won't lie to you, Jessie. I want to see you swollen

and round with our baby inside you. I want you to feel our baby kick. I want to share our child's birth with you. And all the firsts afterward." Tears in his eyes, he stroked her cheek.

He was such a beautiful man. He deserved all those things, even if they could never happen with her. Unable to see his pain any longer, she closed her eyes. "You don't need to say any more, Peter."

"I need you to understand. I want all those things for *us*. I don't want them with anybody but you. Only with you."

"I'm so sorry," she whispered.

"I'm sorry we can't share those important things. But it doesn't change the way I feel about you. It just makes me realize how much I need to be with you."

She sighed, her heart too heavy to do anything else.

"Jessie, I'm so in love with you, I want to share everything with you. I want to celebrate the little family we already have.

"And I need to mourn our loss with you."

"*Our* loss?" She stared into his eyes.

He nodded, his eyes glistening with emotion. "Yours and mine." He looked at her with so much love, she was blinded by it.

Until this moment, she hadn't known what she needed to hear. He understood all he was giving up. All she'd been forced to give up. He understood and shared the loss. The weight on her heart easing, she opened her arms to him.

He folded her gently in his embrace.

He felt wonderful—strong and steady and sure. Tears filling her eyes, she gave herself over to the magic of being in his arms. To the magic of possibilities she'd never dared contemplate.

He pulled back, but only long enough to dip his head and claim her mouth.

She had trouble catching her breath. She'd never felt so much all at once. Her feelings for him were overpowering.

Slowly ending the kiss, he smiled into her eyes. "My life is no longer my own, sweetheart. It belongs to you and Jake. And it is so good to be home."

She hugged him closer.

"Will you marry me, Jessie?" he murmured in her ear. "Soon?"

"Yes. I will marry you. Very soon." Her breath hitched, reality nudging her mind. Madison. His research. Scott and Karen.

Peter was an amazing man who dedicated his life to helping others. She was so fortunate to be loved and needed by such a man. She wanted to marry him and establish a home and family with him. He'd said she and Jake could continue to live in Noah's Crossing.

But loving him called for sacrifices on her part and on his. Loving him meant she needed to open her heart and her life to him in every way. His words came back to her. *...Praying...not so much asking for what you want as asking to be changed in ways you can't imagine.*

Putting her trust in God and Peter, she leaned back to look up at him. "No matter how okay you are with Jake and me continuing to live in Noah's Crossing, I'm not okay with it. I need to move to Madison with my family. You and Jake deserve nothing less. And neither do I."

He frowned. "Are you sure?"

"Yes." She smiled. "It will be a whole new beginning."

He kissed her forehead. "We'll visit often. I promise."

"I'll hold you to that."

His crooked smile peeked through. "Does this mean you've finally come to your senses about me?"

"It means I love you, Peter Sheridan." She stroked his jaw, his whisker stubble prickling her fingers. "And yes, I'm finally coming to my senses about you—about a lot of things. I'm so grateful God sent you to love us."

His handsome face breaking into a grin, he bent and kissed her again.

\* \* \* \* \*

Dear Reader,

I'm so glad you chose Peter and Jessie's story to read. I hope you enjoyed watching them fall in love as they helped each other overcome their problems and learn to trust God. Writing their story was both challenging and part of my own journey in trusting God.

Researching ALS (Lou Gehrig's disease) and learning about the strides researchers are making to find cures for it and other neurological diseases like it was encouraging and healing. ALS and Parkinson's took two of my beloved aunts from us, so you can see why Peter's courage and self-sacrifice make him a hero in my eyes. I hope you found him inspiring, as well.

I'd love to hear your thoughts and feelings about the book. You can write to me at Love Inspired Books, 233 Broadway, Suite 1001, New York, NY 10279, email me at carol@carolvoss.com or visit me on the web at: www.carolvoss.com.

Grace always,

*Carol Voss*

# QUESTIONS FOR DISCUSSION

1. After the accident, Jessie gives up her dreams, moves back with her parents and refuses to consider moving away from Noah's Crossing. Have you ever felt defeated by life's circumstances? If so, what helped you go on?

2. Why does Jessie resent her parents' and friends' concern for her? Have you ever felt resentful over something you knew you should be thankful for? How did you deal with it?

3. Peter is completely dedicated to his research in a race against time to save his friend. Why is it so important to him that he take on the role of daddy, as well?

4. Why does Jessie decide to help Peter with Jake even when she fears Peter could decide to fight her for custody of her baby? Do you understand her decision?

5. What did Peter do to ruin Jessie's budding trust in him? What is his biggest flaw? How did his past contribute?

6. Jessie loves her twin and deeply grieves her death even though she doesn't understand her sister's choices. Have you ever struggled to understand a loved one's choices? Explain.

7. Why is Jessie convinced that any man who loves children will want babies of his own? Do the men in her life contradict her belief? Why or why not?

8. A lifelong Christian, Jessie still struggles with faith. Do you understand her struggle? What is her mother's advice to her? Have you ever questioned your faith? When? What did you do about it?

9. How are Jessie and Peter different in their ways of approaching God? Do you think they are able to help each other in their faiths? If so, how?

10. Do you know anyone who has a debilitating, life-threatening disease? How do you encourage that person?

11. Jessie fears losing people she loves. How does she handle her fear? How do you handle yours?

12. How does Peter overcome his pain? What does he learn over the course of the story? How?

13. *When I am afraid, I will trust in you. —Psalms 56:3* Have you ever had trouble living by these powerful words? Why?

14. Do you believe trusting God is a prerequisite to trusting people? Why or why not?

15. Jessie learns God has a plan for her life that is beyond anything she imagined. Do you believe God has an overall plan for you? Do you know what it is?

# INSPIRATIONAL

Inspirational romances to warm your heart & soul.

*Love Inspired.*

## TITLES AVAILABLE NEXT MONTH

### Available May 31, 2011

**SECOND CHANCE DAD**
*Aspen Creek Crossroads*
**Roxanne Rustand**

**ROCKY POINT REUNION**
**Barbara McMahon**

**AN ACCIDENTAL FAMILY**
*Accidental Blessings*
**Loree Lough**

**THE COWBOY'S HOMECOMING**
**Brenda Minton**

**HOME SWEET HOME**
**Kim Watters**

**SMALL-TOWN HEARTS**
*Men of Allegany County*
**Ruth Logan Herne**